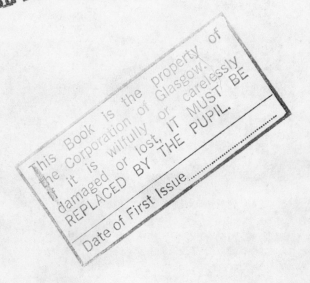

Springboard

Springboard

modern short stories for the middle school

edited by

DAVID JACKSON

*Head of the English Department,
Whitworth Comprehensive School*

with photographs by
JIM COTTRILL

GEORGE G. HARRAP & CO. LTD
London   Toronto   Wellington   Sydney

First published in Great Britain 1970
by GEORGE G. HARRAP & CO. LTD
182 High Holborn, London, W.C.1

SBN 245 59977 0

Printed by offset in Great Britain by
Alden & Mowbray Ltd at the Alden Press, Oxford
Made in Great Britain

To the reader

Do your parents ever seem to have favourites? Have you ever felt ridiculed in front of the class? Have you ever been fooled by the flashy neon sign outside a fairground side-show—and found inside that the "Alligator Woman" was made of plastic, or that the "African Man-eating Lion" was a mangy, tired, flea-bitten creature? Have you ever found out that a person you have hero-worshipped for a long time is really a selfish loud-mouth? Have you ever wanted to varnish your nails bright red?

This is what this book of short stories and pictures is about—fragments of your lives, your thoughts and feelings, which you can use as a springboard into all kinds of activities in the classroom. Why don't you make up a play (improvised or with your own script) based on Bill Naughton's *A Good Sixpenn'orth*? When you have read D. H. Lawrence's *Adolf* find out whether your friends, parents, and teachers think that wild animals should be kept as pets. Tape-record a radio script version of Ray Bradbury's *Zero Hour*, written from the children's point of view—remember all those possibilities for sound effects!

Look closely, too, at the photographs and then write honestly about anything they suggest to you. This is what Fay Lawrenson, aged twelve, wrote about putting lipstick on for the first time:

> Hurriedly she pushes the lipstick back into her sister's
> bag
> And hides her face in a pillow.
> The door opens and a girl enters the bedroom.
> With a small smile
> She picks up her disturbed bag,
> With the words
> "Wash it off, 'fore Mum sees."

Above all, always try to connect the stories and pictures with your own experience, as Fay has done in her poem. You will find that you are able to understand your life and the stories better.

Todmorden, 1969   David Jackson

Contents

A Good Sixpenn'orth

Bill Naughton

Three of us were on our way home from school one January
afternoon when a man with a cigarette-end in his mouth
asked us would we like a job. "I want you to cart this loose
load of coal into that coalshed. It'll be worth a bob," he
added.

"Apiece?" I asked.

"Between you," he said.

It was an enormous heap of large coal gleaming in the
grey light of the back street. We gazed at it for a minute,
and then had a whisper among us. "Make it eighteen-pence,
mister," I suggested, "an' we'll take it on—for then we'll
have a tanner each."

He agreed, and we set to work. Harry Finch filled the
buckets, I ran in with them, and Basher stacked it inside
the shed. The man leant on a broom and flicked an
occasional piece of coal from my path. He kept blowing on
his hands to keep warm. Two hours saw the job done, by
which time the sweat was pouring out of us, and I was
feeling weak in the legs. Then the man knocked on the
back door, and a woman came out and gave him half a
crown. He turned and gave us sixpence each.

"Not much," I said, looking at the little coin in my
blistered hand, "considering you got a bob."

"I'm the contractor," he said. "And don't forget, you'd
have had nothing but for me."

"He's right," agreed Harry and Basher. "And besides,"
went on Harry, "just think of the fun we can have with a
tanner at the Fair. The New Year rush is over, and all the
prices are down, because it travels to-morrow."

"Good idea," I said. "I'll meet you at seven o'clock, an'
we'll go to the Fair and have a right good tanner's worth."

Scrubbed and excited, the three of us met on time and

made off for the Fair. Once clear of the narrow streets and high black factories, we spotted from the main road the strange pale glow like a halo over the Fair. We walked faster, and as we neared the Fairground we were caught by the exciting smells, fragments of blaring music and voices, and by the sense of movement: of roundabouts, big swings, cakewalks, helter-skelters, and whatnot, so that we broke into a trot.

The ground under our feet was slushy, and the glaring lights illuminated an almost deserted Fair. We liked it that way. Our heads stopped reeling, and we were able to stroll about the place and savour the atmosphere without being overcome and spending our money rashly.

"Take it easy," I warned my mates, "and let's keep scouting round till we've found the top value for money."

We watched the Flying Pigs, Big Boats, Bumper Cars, all going cheap, but we clung to our sixpences. We inspected every game of chance and skill: Hoopla, All Press, Dartboards, Ringboards, Roll-a-Penny, Skittles, Bagatelle, Rifle Range, and Coconut Shies.

"Look at that hairy 'un," whispered Harry. "I've allus wanted to knock off a coconut—and I reckon that 'ud drop with a touch.

"That's what you think," I said.

"I vote we have a good feed of them hot peas," said Basher. "Just smell 'em. What you spend on your guts, my Mum reckons, is never lost."

"Don't rush it, Basher," I said.

"A coconut's the best bet," said Harry. "You might even knock *two* off—and they'd last for days."

"We didn't come by our money so easy," I cautioned them, "so let's use our discretion afore we part with it."

At that moment my eye caught sight of the figure of a man in silk shirt and riding-breeches, a silver-handled whip in his hand, poised on a platform beneath the brightest lights on the fairground.

"Ladies and gentlemen," called out a beautiful blonde lady, "Introducing Waldo—the greatest lion-tamer of all time. Any moment now he will enter the cage of Nero!

Nero the Untamable! The African jungle lion that has killed four trainers—the largest lion in Europe—the fiercest in captivity. Waldo will positively enter his cage! Will he come out alive?"

I felt hands tugging me back by the jacket. "Hy, where are you off?" asked Basher.

"Quick," I said, "let's get in afore the crowd."

"What crowd?" asked Harry.

"One small coin, ladies and gentlemen, sixpence only, brings you the greatest thrill of all time!"

"Keep still," hissed Basher.

"Get your tanners ready," I said, "we can't afford to miss it."

"No, you don't," said Basher. "Black peas, a whacking great plateful for tuppence, an' finish off with roasted spuds."

"Big hairy coconuts," whispered Harry.

I couldn't take my eyes off Waldo, unsmiling and unafraid. He bowed to us, stepped from the platform, and disappeared. Before Basher and Harry could hold me I was at the paybox.

"Half, please."

"*Half?* Why, you're going in for a *quarter* to-night. Two bob's the proper price.... You don't expect to see a chap eaten by a lion for threepence?"

I handed over the sixpence. I waved to my mates, but they wouldn't come. So I quickly went inside the tent, so as to get near the front. Inside were four people, and they looked at me pityingly. There was a well-dressed couple, an old man, and a woman who looked like a Sunday school teacher. It was very cold, and after the bright lights outside one could only see dimly. I went and stood near the stage.

There was no sign of Waldo. After a long time I heard the beating of a drum and the woman announcer. I felt like going out again and listening.

"We can't wait much longer," I heard the man say to the woman. "Is he never going to go in to that wretched beast?"

Only five more people came in during the next twenty

9

minutes. I felt chilled, and I was aware of an empty spot of skin in the palm of my hand, where I had clutched the sixpence. Then there was a final beating of the drum, and Waldo appeared on the stage before me.

His face was all powdered, and there was a smell of stale beer off him. He looked at us with disgust. And then the announcer bustled in. The curtain was pulled open, and there was a cage. Lying in the nearest corner was a big lion. It was less than a yard away from me, and it blinked its eyes and gave a good-tempered yawn.

"During the act, ladies and gentlemen, there must be complete silence. One sound, and Waldo may never come out alive. His life is in your hands. Since no insurance company will insure Waldo's life, I ask any of you who can afford it to place an extra coin in the hat. Thank you!"

Waldo cracked his whip outside the cage, and Nero slowly got to his feet. The woman took a revolver out of her pocket. Waldo went to the door of the cage, and sprang back when the lion came. This seemed to disturb the lion. As it moved away Waldo quickly opened the cage and darted inside. He cracked the whip, and Nero loped wearily round the cage. He went after it, cracking the whip over his head. *"Silence!"* called the announcer. Nero skipped round the cage for about two minutes, then sank down to rest in the same corner. Waldo leapt to the door, opened it, and got out. Nero never moved. It looked at me again, blinked, sighed, and rested.

"Ladies and gentlemen," called the blonde announcer, putting away the revolver, "that concludes the performance."

I couldn't believe it.

I exchanged one last look with the lion as the curtain was drawn across the stage. I even clapped feebly with the others. And the next thing I was outside.

"Look!" shouted Harry Finch. "That shaggy 'un—I knocked it off." He dangled an enormous coconut before my eyes.

"Black peas an' roasted spuds," sighed Basher. "Here"—he grabbed my head and pressed my ear against his fat, warm stomach—"can you hear 'em churning about inside?

Luv'ly."

Harry shook the coconut against my ear. "Fair loaded with milk. I knocked it clean off with the last ball. A right good tanner's worth."

"Not as good as mine," said Basher. "First I had a plate of hot peas, then a bag of roasted spuds, an' then another plate of hot peas."

The image of old Nero seemed fastened before my eyes; the smell of the lion, the sleepy old head, and gentle blinking eyes. *The fiercest lion in captivity.* We went walking along the streets homeward.

"How was the lion-taming show?" they asked at last.

"Champion," I said. "Worth anybody's money."

"You've not had much to say about it," remarked Harry, suspiciously.

"Yes, you've kept your trap shut," accused Basher.

"It were that exciting," I said, "as it took my breath away."

"Something did," they said.

I longed to tell them, to unload the misery of my heart, but I dared not. I'd never have lived it down if I had.

"Sorry, lads," I said, "but I've got to be in early." And I ran off home.

I slept badly that night. Next morning when I was on my way to school Harry Finch called out, "He's here, Mum!"

"What's up?" I asked.

"Haven't you heard?" he said.

"Heard what?" I said.

"Waldo the Lion-tamer has been badly mauled by that wild lion. It's on the front page of the *Dispatch.* I told me mum an' she wants to ask you about it."

Out came Mrs Finch with her spectacles on and the *Dispatch* in her hand. "Ee, luv, they says he's in a critical condition—"

"Let's have a look, please," I said to Mrs Finch. It was true. The lion had mauled him! I gave her the paper back. "I'm not surprised," I said, "the way that lion went at him. It clawed the blinking shirt off his back. He could hardly

11

hold it at bay with his whip, an' a woman with a revolver was about to shoot it."

"Ee, suffering Simon! An' did you see all that?"

"'Course I did. Your Harry had a coconut instead."

By this time a few neighbours were at their doors, and when I went off there was a crowd of lads all wanting to hear about Waldo and Nero. I described the powerful physique of Waldo, and the beauty of the woman with the revolver, and told of the wild roaring lion that tried to claw at me through the bars. The school whistle made us run, but in the classroom they began to whisper questions to me. Teacher told me to stop talking.

"Please, miss," said Harry, "it isn't his fault. He was telling me about seeing Waldo the Lion-tamer all but torn to bits last night."

"Is that the person who was so severely mauled?" she asked. "Then you'd better come in front and tell us all."

I went to the front of the classroom and began. "The lion was making furious deep-throated roars even before Waldo attempted to get into the cage. And when it caught sight of him in his blue silk shirt it went into a fury. I was very close to the cage, and when its huge body hit the bars it made the whole tent shudder. The roars were blood-curdling."

Suddenly the class door opened and in came Mr Victor, the headmaster. I was going back to my place, but he called me out again. "Oh, I must hear this—please continue."

I began all over again, adding any new bits that came to mind, when suddenly there was a knock on the door and a monitor ushered in Major Platt, the Inspector of Schools.

"I'm afraid I've interrupted something," he said.

"Not at all, Major," said Mr Victor hurriedly. "It just happens that this boy was present at the fairground performance last evening when the lion-tamer was so badly mauled."

"My goodness, I must hear this!" exclaimed Major Platt. All three of them sat down, and I stepped back a foot to stand on the teacher's platform. I felt in fine form.

"After three attempts to enter the cage the lady with the

12

pearl-handled revolver tried to dissuade the Great Waldo, but he refused to give up, and I heard him say, 'The show must go on.' Then, by a ruse, he got Nero away from the door, and the next moment was inside. The iron door slammed after him. He was alone in the cage with the African man-eating lion. A mighty roar rended the air at that moment, and the big crowd shuddered. Waldo attempted bravely to keep the lion down with his whip—but it gave one spring. The next moment I saw his silk shirt fall to shreds on the floor. But he was unhurt. He drove it into a corner—again it sprang. The woman darted to the bars with the revolver, but I heard Waldo shout, 'Don't shoot!' His eye never left that of the lion. For a long time it parried, trying to knock the whip from his hand. Then at last it succeeded, and again it sprang with an angry roar. Waldo fell to the floor. But in a trice he was clear. But he couldn't get to the door of the cage. And he had lost his whip. The lion seemed to be sizing him up. Then, just as it was about to spring, he snatched a piece of shirt from the floor and waved it in front of its face. When it sprang he was already at the door. The blonde lady unfastened it. Just in the nick of time he got out. Then I noticed a line of blood across his bare back. The entire place trembled as the lion hit the door. Waldo could scarcely stand up. I was right up in front of the crowd. He gave a bow to the audience, and then the lady helped him away. The audience clapped like mad. The lion snarled with fury. Then I went out to meet my mates. One was eating hot peas. The other had knocked off a hairy coconut."

Major Platt, smiling solemnly, or so it seemed to me, patted me on the head. "One day, my boy," he said, "you will make a true journalist." And he slipped a thick, heavy coin into my fist.

Modestly I went back to my place between Harry and Basher. Their eyes fastened enviously on me, and I couldn't resist opening my hand and letting them glimpse the half-crown. They let out a gasp. And Harry grunted, "The lion turned out the best sixpenn'orth after all."

As I sat down I felt the excitement drain away, and

Harry's words brought up a picture of the real Nero before me. I saw the two old eyes of Nero, so weary and worn, and I wondered at the agony it must have suffered to provoke its old jungle temper. In fact, I had half a mind to go out and confess the truth before the entire class. I felt that was the right thing to do. And I would have done it—only, I was a bit scared Major Platt might have taken the half-crown back.

Zero Hour

Ray Bradbury

Oh, it was to be so jolly! What a game! Such excitement they hadn't known in years. The children catapulted this way and that across the green lawns, shouting at each other, holding hands, flying in circles, climbing trees, laughing. Overhead the rockets flew, and beetle cars whispered by on the streets, but the children played on. Such fun, such tremulous joy, such tumbling and hearty screaming.

Mink ran into the house, all dirt and sweat. For her seven years she was loud and strong and definite. Her mother, Mrs Morris, hardly saw her as she yanked out drawers and rattled pans and tools into a large sack.

"Heavens, Mink, what's going on?"

"The most exciting game ever!" gasped Mink, pink-faced.

"Stop and get your breath." said the mother.

"No, I'm all right," gasped Mink. "Okay I take these things, Mom?"

"But don't dent them," said Mrs Morris.

"Thank you, thank you!" cried Mink, and boom! she was gone, like a rocket.

Mrs Morris surveyed the fleeing tot. "What's the name of the game?"

"Invasion!" said Mink. The door slammed.

In every yard on the street children brought out knives and forks and pokers and old stovepipes and can openers.

It was an interesting fact that this fury and bustle occurred only among the younger children. The older ones, those ten years and more, disdained the affair and marched scornfully off on hikes or played a more dignified version of hide-and-seek on their own.

Meanwhile, parents came and went in chromium beetles.

15

Repairmen came to repair the vacuum elevators in houses, to fix fluttering television sets, or hammer upon stubborn food-delivery tubes. The adult civilization passed and repassed the busy youngsters, jealous of the fierce energy of the wild tots, tolerantly amused at their flourishings, longing to join in themselves.

"This and this and *this,*" said Mink, instructing the others with their assorted spoons and wrenches. "Do that, and bring *that* over here. No! *Here,* ninny! Right. Now, get back while I fix this." Tongue in teeth, face wrinkled in thought. "Like that. See?"

"Yayyy!" shouted the kids.

Twelve-year-old Joseph Connors ran up.

"Go away," said Mink straight at him.

"I wanna play," said Joseph.

"Can't!" said Mink.

"Why not?"

"You'd just make fun of us."

"Honest, I wouldn't."

"No. We know *you.* Go away or we'll kick you."

Another twelve-year-old boy whirred by on little motor skates. "Hey, Joe! Come on! Let them sissies play!"

Joseph showed reluctance and a certain wistfulness. "I *want* to play," he said.

"You're old," said Mink firmly.

"Not *that* old," said Joe sensibly.

"You'd only laugh and spoil the Invasion."

The boy on the motor skates made a rude lip noise. "Come on, Joe! Them and their fairies! Nuts!"

Joseph walked off slowly. He kept looking back, all down the block.

Mink was already busy again. She made a kind of apparatus with her gathered equipment. She had appointed another little girl with a pad and pencil to take down notes in painful slow scribbles. Their voices rose and fell in the warm sunlight.

All around them the city hummed. The streets were lined with good green and peaceful trees. Only the wind made a conflict across the city, across the country, across the continent. In a thousand other cities there were trees and children and avenues, businessmen in their quiet offices taping their voices, or watching televisors. Rockets hovered like darning needles in the blue sky. There was the universal, quiet conceit and easiness of men accustomed to peace, quite certain there would never be trouble again. Arm in arm, men all over earth were a united front. The perfect weapons were held in equal trust by all nations. A situation of incredibly beautiful balance had been brought about. There were no traitors among men, no unhappy ones, no disgruntled ones; therefore the world was based upon a stable ground. Sunlight illumined half the world and the trees drowsed in a tide of warm air.

Mink's mother, from her upstairs window, gazed down. The children. She looked upon them and shook her head. Well, they'd eat well, sleep well, and be in school on Monday. Bless their vigorous little bodies. She listened.

Mink talked earnestly to someone near the rose bush— though there was no one there.

These odd children. And the little girl, what was her name? Anna? Anna took notes on a pad. First, Mink asked the rosebush a question, then called the answer to Anna.

"Triangle," said Mink.

"What's a tri," said Anna with difficulty, "angle?"

"Never mind," said Mink.

"How you spell it?" asked Anna.

"T-r-i——" spelled Mink slowly, then snapped, "Oh, spell it yourself!" She went on to other words. "Beam," she said.

"I haven't got tri," said Anna, "angle down yet!"

"Well, hurry, hurry!" cried Mink.

Mink's mother leaned out the upstairs window. "A-n-g-l-e," she spelled down at Anna.

"Oh, thanks Mrs Morris," said Anna.

"Certainly," said Mink's mother and withdrew, laughing, to dust the hall with an electro-duster magnet.

The voices wavered on the shimmery air. "Beam," said Anna. Fading.

"Four-nine-seven-A-and-B-and-X," said Mink, far away,

17

seriously. "And a fork and a string and a–hex-hex-agony–hexagonal!"

At lunch Mink gulped milk at one toss and was at the door. Her mother slapped the table.

"You sit right back down," commanded Mrs Morris. "Hot soup in a minute." She poked a red button on the kitchen butler, and ten seconds later something landed with a bump in the rubber receiver. Mrs Morris opened it, took out a can with a pair of aluminum holders, unsealed it with a flick, and poured hot soup into a bowl.

During all this Mink fidgeted. "Hurry, Mom! This is a matter of life and death! Aw——"

"I was the same way at your age. Always life and death. I know."

Mink banged away at the soup.

"Slow down," said Mom.

"Can't," said Mink. "Drill's waiting for me."

"Who's Drill? What a peculiar name," said Mom.

"You don't know him," said Mink.

"A new boy in the neighborhood?" asked Mom.

"He's new all right," said Mink. She started on her second bowl.

"Which one is Drill?" asked Mom.

"He's around," said Mink evasively. "You'll make fun. Everybody pokes fun. Gee, darn."

"Is Drill shy?"

"Yes. No. In a way. Gosh, Mom, I got to run if we want to have the Invasion!"

"Who's invading what?"

"Martians invading Earth. Well, not exactly Martians. They're–I don't know. From up." She pointed with her spoon.

"And *inside*," said Mom, touching Mink's feverish brow.

Mink rebelled. "You're laughing! You'll kill Drill and everybody."

"I didn't mean to," said Mom. "Drill's a Martian?"

"No. He's–well–maybe from Jupiter or Saturn or Venus. Anyway, he's had a hard time."

"I imagine." Mrs Morris hid her mouth behind her hand.

18

"They couldn't figure a way to attack Earth."

"We're impregnable," said Mom in mock seriousness.

"That's the word Drill used! Impreg—— That was the word, Mom."

"My, my, Drill's a brilliant little boy. Two-bit words."

"They couldn't figure a way to attack, Mom. Drill says—he says in order to make a good fight you got to have a new way of surprising people. That way you win. And he says also you got to have help from your enemy."

"A fifth column," said Mom.

"Yeah. That's what Drill said. And they couldn't figure a way to surprise Earth or get help."

"No wonder. We're pretty darn strong." Mom laughed, cleaning up. Mink sat there, staring at the table, seeing what she was talking about.

"Until, one day," whispered Mink melodramatically. "they thought of children!"

"Well!" said Mrs Morris brightly.

"And they thought of how grownups are so busy they never look under rosebushes or on lawns!"

"Only for snails and fungus."

"And then there's something about dim-dims."

"Dim-dims?"

"Dimens-shuns."

"Dimensions?"

"Four of 'em! And there's something about kids under nine and imagination. It's real funny to hear Drill talk."

Mrs Morris was tired. "Well, it must be funny. You're keeping Drill waiting now. It's getting late in the day and, if you want to have your Invasion before your supper bath, you'd better jump."

"Do I have to take a bath?" growled Mink.

"You do. Why is it children hate water? No matter what age you live in children hate water behind the ears!"

"Drill says I won't have to take baths," said Mink.

"Oh, he does, does he?"

"He told all the kids that. No more baths. And we can stay up till ten o'clock and go to two televisor shows on Saturday 'stead of one!"

"Well, Mr Drill better mind his p's and q's. I'll call up his mother and——"

Mink went to the door. "We're having trouble with guys like Pete Britz and Dale Jerrick. They're growing up. They make fun. They're worse than parents. They just won't believe in Drill. They're so snooty, 'cause they're growing up. You'd think they'd know better. They were little only a coupla years ago. I hate them worst. We'll kill them *first*."

"Your father and I last?"

"Drill says you're dangerous. Know why? 'Cause you don't believe in Martians! They're going to let *us* run the world. Well, not just us, but the kids over in the next block, too. I might be queen." She opened the door.

"Mom?"

"Yes?"

"What's lodge-ick?"

"Logic? Why, dear, logic is knowing what things are true and not true."

"He *mentioned* that," said Mink. "And what's im-pression-able?" It took her a minute to say it.

"Why, it means——" Her mother looked at the floor, laughing gently. "It means–to be a child, dear."

"Thanks for lunch!" Mink ran out, then stuck her head back in. "Mom, I'll be sure you won't be hurt much, really!"

"Well, thanks," said Mom.

Slam went the door.

At four o'clock the audiovisor buzzed. Mrs Morris flipped the tab. "Hello, Helen!" she said in welcome.

"Hello, Mary. How are things in New York?"

"Fine. How are things in Scranton? You look tired."

"So do you. The children. Underfoot," said Helen.

Mrs Morris sighed. "My Mink too. The super-Invasion."

Helen laughed. "Are your kids playing that game too?"

"Lord, yes. Tomorrow it'll be geometrical jacks and motorized hopscotch. Were we this bad when we were kids in '48?"

"Worse. Japs and Nazis. Don't know how my parents

put up with me. Tomboy."

"Parents learn to shut their ears."

A silence.

"What's wrong, Mary?" asked Helen.

Mrs Morris's eyes were half closed; her tongue slid slowly, thoughtfully, over her lower lip. "Eh?" She jerked. "Oh, nothing. Just thought about *that.* Shutting ears and such. Never mind. Where were we?"

"My boy Tim's got a crush on some guy named—*Drill,* I think it was."

"Must be a new password. Mink likes him too."

"Didn't know it had got as far as New York. Word of mouth, I imagine. Looks like a scrap drive. I talked to Josephine and she said her kids—that's in Boston—are wild on this new game. It's sweeping the country."

At that moment Mink trotted into the kitchen to gulp a glass of water. Mrs Morris turned. "How're things going?"

"Almost finished," said Mink.

"Swell," said Mrs Morris. "What's *that?*"

"A yo-yo," said Mink. "Watch."

She flung the yo-yo down its string. Reaching the end it—

It vanished.

"See?" said Mink. "Ope!" Dibbling her finger, she made the yo-yo reappear and zip up the string.

"Do that again," said her mother.

"Can't. Zero hour's five o'clock! 'By." Mink exited, zipping her yo-yo.

On the audiovisor, Helen laughed. "Tim brought one of those yo-yos in this morning, but when I got curious he said he wouldn't show it to me, and when I tried to work it, finally, it wouldn't work."

"You're not *impressionable*," said Mrs Morris.

"What?"

"Never mind. Something I thought of. Can I help you, Helen?"

"I wanted to get that black-and-white cake recipe——"

The hour drowsed by. The day waned. The sun lowered

21

in the peaceful blue sky. Shadows lengthened on the green lawns. The laughter and excitement continued. One little girl ran away, crying. Mrs Morris came out the front door.

"Mink, was that Peggy Ann crying?"

Mink was bent over in the yard, near the rosebush. "Yeah. She's a scarebaby. We won't let her play, now. She's getting too old to play. I guess she grew up all of a sudden."

"Is that why she cried? Nonsense. Give me a civil answer, young lady, or inside you come!"

Mink whirled in consternation, mixed with irritation. "I can't quit now. It's almost time. I'll be good. I'm sorry."

"Did you hit Peggy Ann?"

"No, honest. You ask her. It was something—well, she's just a scaredy pants."

The ring of children drew in around Mink where she scowled at her work with spoons and a kind of square-shaped arrangement of hammers and pipes. "There and there," murmured Mink.

"What's wrong?" said Mrs Morris.

"Drill's stuck. Halfway. If we could only get him all the way through, it'd be easier. Then all the others could come through after him."

"Can I help?"

"No'm, thanks. I'll fix it."

"All right. I'll call you for your bath in half an hour. I'm tired of watching you."

She went in and sat in the electric relaxing chair, sipping a little beer from a half-empty glass. The chair massaged her back. Children, children. Children and love and hate, side by side. Sometimes children loved you, hated you—all in half a second. Strange children, did they ever forget or forgive the whippings and the harsh, strict words of command? She wondered. How can you ever forget or forgive those over and above you, those tall and silly dictators?

Time passed. A curious, waiting silence came upon the streets, deepening.

Five o'clock. A clock sang softly somewhere in the

22

house in a quiet, musical voice: "Five o'clock—five o'clock. Time's a-wasting. Five o'clock," and purred away into silence.

Zero hour.

Mrs Morris chuckled in her throat. Zero hour.

A beetle car hummed into the driveway. Mr Morris. Mrs Morris smiled. Mr Morris got out of the beetle, locked it and called hello to Mink at her work. Mink ignored him. He laughed and stood for a moment watching the children. Then he walked up the front steps.

"Hello, darling."

"Hello, Henry."

She strained forward on the edge of the chair, listening. The children were silent. Too silent.

He emptied his pipe, refilled it. "Swell day. Makes you glad to be alive."

Buzz.

"What's that?" asked Henry.

"I don't know. She got up suddenly, her eyes widening. She was going to say something. She stopped it. Ridiculous. Her nerves jumped. "Those children haven't anything dangerous out there, have they?" she said.

"Nothing but pipes and hammers. Why?"

"Nothing electrical?"

"Heck, no," said Henry. "I looked."

She walked to the kitchen. The buzzing continued. "Just the same, you'd better go tell them to quit. It's after five. Tell them——" Her eyes widened and narrowed. "Tell them to put off their Invasion until tomorrow." She laughed, nervously.

The buzzing grew louder.

"What are they up to? I'd better go look, all right."

The explosion!

The house shook with dull sound. There were other explosions in other yards on other streets.

Involuntarily, Mrs Morris screamed. "Up this way!" she cried senselessly, knowing no sense, no reason. Perhaps she saw something from the corners of her eyes; perhaps she smelled a new odour or heard a new noise. There was no time to argue with Henry to convince him. Let him think her insane. Yes, insane! Shrieking, she ran upstairs. He ran after her to see what she was up to. "In the attic!" she screamed. "That's where it is!" It was only a poor excuse to get him in the attic in time. Oh, God—in time!

Another explosion outside. The children screamed with delight as if at a great fireworks display.

"It's not in the attic!" cried Henry. "It's outside!"

"No, no!" Wheezing, gasping, she fumbled at the attic door. "I'll show you. Hurry! I'll show you!"

They tumbled into the attic. She slammed the door, locked it, took the key, threw it into a far, cluttered corner.

She was babbling wild stuff now. It came out of her. All the subconscious suspicion and fear that had gathered secretly all afternoon and fermented like a wine in her. All the little revelations and knowledges and sense that had bothered her all day and which she had logically and carefully and sensibly rejected and censored. Now it exploded in her and shook her to bits.

"There, there," she said, sobbing against the door. "We're safe until tonight. Maybe we can sneak out. Maybe we can escape!"

Henry blew up too, but for another reason. "Are you crazy? Why'd you throw that key away? Blast it!"

"Yes, yes, I'm crazy, if it helps, but stay here with me!"

"I don't know how I can get out!"

"Quiet. They'll hear us. Oh, God, they'll find us soon enough——"

Below them, Mink's voice. The husband stopped. There was a great universal humming and sizzling, a screaming and giggling. Downstairs the audio-televisor buzzed and buzzed insistently, alarmingly, violently. *Is that Helen calling?* thought Mrs Morris. *And is she calling about what I think she's calling about?*

Footsteps came into the house. Heavy footsteps.

"Who's coming in my house?" demanded Henry angrily. "Who's tramping around down there?"

Heavy feet. Twenty, thirty, forty, fifty of them. Fifty persons crowding into the house. The humming. The

24

giggling of the children. "This way!" cried Mink, below.

"Who's downstairs?" roared Henry. "Who's there!"

"Hush. Oh, nononononono!" said his wife, weakly, holding him. "Please, be quiet. They might go away."

"Mom?" called Mink. "Dad?" A pause. "Where are you?"

Heavy footsteps, heavy, heavy, *very heavy* footsteps, came up the stairs. Mink leading them.

"Mom?" A hesitation. "Dad?" A waiting, a silence. Humming. Footsteps toward the attic. Mink's first.

They trembled together in silence in the attic, Mr and Mrs Morris. For some reason the electric humming, the queer cold light suddenly visible under the door crack, the strange odour, and the alien sound of eagerness in Mink's voice finally got through to Henry Morris too. He stood, shivering, in the dark silence, his wife beside him.

"Mom! Dad!"

Footsteps. A little humming sound. The attic lock melted. The door opened. Mink peered inside, tall blue shadows behind her.

"Peekaboo," said Mink.

The Mersey Look

Eric Allen

The old man was just an old man with a fuzzy beard. Roddy had noticed him standing there by the edge of the pond, watching while the bread-crumb lady gave the gulls their breakfast. There were ducks there, too, with green heads, hundreds of them. They pushed their way greedily in front of the gulls and fussed up and down, making a noise like pulling your wet finger along a tight-stretched rubber inner tube. But the bread-crumb lady always threw the bread-crumbs as far out as she could, so that only the gulls got them. The old man had stood there nodding his head, as if he approved of this. Then after a little while Roddy had gone away, round to the other side of the pond, to sail his boat.

Roddy's boat wasn't a sailing yacht, like those that most of the kids brought to the pond. It was a Dutch barge with a broad flat bottom and dark brown sails, and a Dutch flag. It didn't sail very well because of its lack of a keel. Instead it had sort of flipper things at the sides that swivelled up and down and that helped to keep it from turning turtle too often when it was in the water. But it wasn't in the water now. Roddy had put it down on a seat just by the place where the pigeons came to paddle. He was poking at one of the pigeons with his long cane when the old man spoke to him.

"What's the matter, then?" the old man said. "Don't you like pigeons?"

Roddy turned his head and looked, but he didn't speak.

"You'll drown them pigeons if you don't watch it," the old man went on. "Pigeons ain't ducks, you know, nor gulls either. Pigeons can't swim."

But Roddy knew better than that. "Yes they can swim," he said. "If you poke them far enough out they swim all

26

right. They just like to keep their feet on the bottom, that's all."

The old man seemed not to hear. The boat lying on the seat had caught his attention now. He went over to have a closer look at it.

"That's a bom boat you got there," he said. "A Dutch bom boat. You'll find lots of them, Holland way. Is she yours, then? Where did you get her?"

"I got it for Christmas," Roddy said. "My dad brought it back. It's a barge."

"A barge!" The old man gave a somewhat jeering laugh. "That's no barge. That's a bom boat, I tell you. Ain't you ever been to the Science Museum, then? They've got 'em there. In glass cases they've got 'em. You want to go and look. It's not far. Just a bit of a step across the park here. You wouldn't call this craft no barge any more. She's a bomboat. A Dutch bom boat."

Roddy didn't need to be told where the Sciende Museum was. And in any case he knew what a barge looked like without going there. But he wasn't really listening to what the old man was saying, only to the way that he was saying it. You could tell that he wasn't from London by the way he talked: he talked the way some of the policemen in 'Z Cars' did. Roddy waited until the old man had finished, then he asked:

"Do you come from the Mersey?"

The old man gave him a swift, sharp look... a Mersey look.

"It's the way you talk," Roddy went on, "like the Rascals or someone."

"The Rascals," repeated the old man, sharply. He sucked thoughtfully at one of his teeth. "Them with the hair, you mean?" He was looking Roddy up and down, taking him in—the red pullover and blue jeans and what he could see of the Canadian lumberjack shirt. Finally he said, "You could do with a bit of a haircut yourself if it comes to that," and then turned away, back to where Roddy's boat lay on the seat.

Roddy flushed, and ran his fingers through his hair. He was tired of being told that he needed a haircut. Old Wilson

27

at school had had him out in front of the class about it, just before they had broken up for Christmas. He had tried to explain, that it was the look—the Mersey look. You didn't go to a barber just to have your hair cut, like kids did: you went to have it styled. But it was no use talking. They never even tried to see it your way.

He looked across towards the seat where the old man was fiddling with the sail of the boat in a shy sort of way—as if he were too shy to have a real thorough go at whatever he thought wanted doing. As he watched, Roddy had the strange idea that... Well, it was like the way little kids would sometimes stand around when you were doing something, just itching to be asked to lend a hand. The thought made him frown. Well, he wasn't going to ask this old codger to help him sail the boat if that's what he thought, not after what he had just said about his hair and that.

But apparently the old man had nothing of the sort in mind, for he turned to Roddy now and said, "She'll never sail. She'll never get across the pond here, not from one side to the other, do you know that?"

As a matter of fact Roddy did know it. More than once he had hung anxiously about the edge of the pond for hours and hours, missing his tea, and getting into a proper row at home, while he waited for his boat to come drifting slowly in, bottom upwards. He wasn't going to admit it though, not to this old man who seemed to think that he knew it all anyway. So he said, "I... I've got to get along home now... for my dinner."

"Your dinner?" The old man shot him another of those swift, sharp looks. "You have your dinner early, don't you? Can't be more than a couple of hours since you had your breakfast."

Roddy couldn't think of anything more to say. He went over to the seat and took up his boat. It should have been easy enough just to walk off, but somehow it wasn't. He stood for a couple of minutes, pretending to be doing something to the bowsprit or whatever it was that the sail joined to along the bottom.

"Well..." said the old man. "Better come on, then, if

you're coming, hadn't you? I'll walk you as far as the gate."

Roddy hadn't really meant to leave the park at all. It was a marvellous day for boat sailing, except that there wasn't any wind... though that was even better really, for his boat, since it was the wind that blew it over. When there was no wind you could push it along round the edge of the pond like anything, and so long as no kids or dogs got in the way you could pretend that it really was a real barge on a genuine Dutch canal.

He walked along for a bit, thinking about it. Then he began to think about the great big sailing yachts that the men raced on the pond on Sunday mornings. There had been a time when he had wanted one of those more than anything, with a mast higher than himself and a thing for working the rudder so that the boat went the way you wanted it to instead of round and round in circles like the kids' yachts did. But then on Sunday a man had turned up with a motor-boat that went twice as fast as any of the yachts and that made even the swans hurry up to get out of the way.

"Do you like boats, then?" he heard the old man say to him.

And then he heard himself saying, "Yes. Yes, I do."

Well... and so he did, in a way. There wasn't anything not to like about them, was there?... Except falling off one, maybe, and getting wet.

"And ships, too," the old man went on, though really as if he were talking to himself. "Ships and the sea."

Roddy didn't like to tell him that he had never actually been on a ship. He nearly had once, when his form had gone to Paris for Easter, but his dad had just got laid off at the works and so he hadn't been able to go.

They had come to the gates of the park. Roddy stopped.

"Which way do you go now, then?" the old man asked.

Roddy pointed. "That way."

"Ah. That's my way, too. I'll walk along with you a bit, then, shall I?"

There ought to be some way of saying no, Roddy thought. If any of the lads saw him they would make a proper game of it afterwards. But when he got as far as the traffic lights he would say that he had to meet his mum outside Woolworths. Then when the old man had gone he would slip back to the pond again with his boat.

"Will you be wanting to go to sea, then, when you leave school?" the old man asked him as they turned away from the park gates and walked together along the busy main road.

"I... I don't know," said Roddy. "I might."

But he did know—he knew perfectly well. When he left school he was going to sing with a group, like the Rascals, and make a golden disc and everything, and have crowds of people waiting outside his house for him to come out. The only thing was that he couldn't really sing much—not yet. He might do better when his voice broke, though. Even if he didn't he could still be a guitar player, the greatest: he simply had to practise and practise... as soon as he got his guitar.

The music shop on the corner by the traffic lights had a window full of them. There were tape-recorders in the window, too, and records. They had the Rascals' latest L.P., and a great big picture of them, signed Alan, and Colin, and Sid. When the old man had gone, he promised himself, he would cross over and have a look.

But then just as they were coming to the lights the old man said to him, suddenly, "I got something I want to show you... just down here."

Roddy knew that he ought to say no, that he had to meet his mum; and that was what he wanted to say. But it was all so unexpected. The old man had taken his arm and was leading him down the turning by the cinema before he had a chance to say anything at all.

"It's right here," the old man said to him. "On the corner here. That's my shop."

Roddy knew the shop. He had often looked into its single small window, so encrusted with dirt that you could hardly see in, and wondered who would want to buy old door-knobs and bits of lead pipe and brass water-taps gone green and all the rest of the junk with which the window was crammed. He had never seen anyone go into the shop. Indeed, they couldn't go in, even if they wanted to, since the door was always locked.

It was locked now. That was, it had been. But the old man had fumbled around in his pocket and found a bunch of keys, and now he had the door open and was holding it back for Roddy to go through.

It was dark inside the shop, and there were old prams and oil-drums and a great brass bedstead piled everywhere. But the old man didn't stop. He led the way across and into a room at the back, where he switched on a light.

'Come in, then. Come on in," he invited. "Don't stand out there. There ain't no charge to come in. Here, put your boat down on there. It won't hurt."

Roddy didn't put his boat down. He stood just inside the doorway, looking about him. The room was small, and was filled up mostly with a carpenter's bench that was littered with all sorts of chisels and carving tools and bits of wood and tobacco-tins with nails in them, and a glue-pot and a gas-ring to heat the glue on, and piles and piles of old cotton-reels and cigar-boxes, and in the middle of it all the half-finished model of a sailing-ship with two masts already up and a third lying there on the bench waiting to be fixed.

It wasn't the only model in the room. There was another on a shelf, all covered in dust, only this was of the sort of ship that Columbus went to America on. And then there was one in a glass case, like the *Victory,* but instead of being made of wood, made of bone. There were pictures of ships, too, all round the room, not framed, but pinned up with thumb tacks, and there were piles of books about ships, too, all mixed up with the sawdust and shavings that from the look of it must have littered the floor for years and years.

"Well?" the old man said. He seemed suddenly to look a lot younger, Roddy thought. His eyes were happy, and he was rubbing his hands together. "Well, what do you think? Isn't she lovely, eh?"

Roddy went up to the bench for a closer look at the

31

unfinished model. It was marvellous. Every tiny little bit was exactly like the real thing. There were rings like those on umbrellas, only painted white, for lifebelts, and real glass windows that you could see through, and the deck was just like real, too, made of planks.

The old man was standing by him, explaining things, "That's what I use the cigar-boxes for, you see," he was saying. "I cut 'em into strips for the deck. And I always carve the blocks out of bone so as the rigging'll run free."

"Did you make it all yourself, then?" Roddy asked. "Did you really make it?"

"Aye," the old man nodded. "I've been working on her for a year and a half now. Won't be so long before she's finished."

"I'll bet you'll be glad when she is," said Roddy.

"Well, I don't know about that," the old man answered. "I will, but then again I won't. I've been making model ships for more than thirty years. You should have seen the first one I tried my hand at. Proper ashamed of that one I'd be now. But this here... well, I've waited. I waited a long time before I started on her."

The old man crossed to the wall at the back of the workroom. There was a picture of a sailing-ship there. This one was in a frame. He hooked it down and carried it over to where Roddy stood, blowing dust from the glass as he came.

"That's her," the old man said. "The *Margaret Macann...* and a smarter hooker than she never sailed from the Mersey. 'Course, I spent most of my time in steam, but the old *Meg Macann* didn't make her last voyage till 1897. She was about the last of the old windjammers and she hung on just long enough for me to sail on her for half a year as ship's boy. I couldn't have been more than a year or two older than you are yourself at the time."

"Gee!" said Roddy. "Did you really sail on her, then? Did you go to China?"

"China?" The old man laughed. "No, I didn't get to China till afterwards. New Zealand we was bound for, and back again with wool. But coming up into the Irish Sea, it was as if old Meg knew that there was nothing waiting for

her but the shipbreaker's yard. She put us ashore off David's Head as neat and clean as could be, and then just turned over in her bed, as you might say, and sank."

When Roddy did at last get home his mother said to him, "Well, here's a nice time to come marching in, I must say. Thought you'd fallen in the pond. I was just sending out to look for you."

Roddy mumbled something, and then went into the kitchen to get his dried-up shepherd's pie from the oven. While he ate he answered his mother's questions in grunts, or not at all, until she gave it up and left him there at the kitchen table, his head full of halyards and dead-eyes and fore and aft rigged schooners, and the difference between clinker-built craft and carvel-built, and why a lugger was called a lugger, and what it meant to sail on a taut bowline, or close-hauled, into the wind.

When his dad came home that night, and his mother said something about his having been down at the round pond half the day with that barge of his, Roddy answered quickly that it wasn't a barge, but a bom boat.

"I'm going to the Science Museum tomorrow," he said. "They've got lots of them there, in glass cases, and all sorts of other boats too."

It was the start of something new, and as always with Roddy he plunged right into it up to the eyebrows.

"It won't last, you know," his mother said to his father. "It's just one of his crazes."

But this didn't stop Roddy going up to the little junk shop every morning right through the holidays, and peering through the dirty window to see if there was a light in the work-room at the back. If there was he would kick the door until Mr Nixon, as his old man was called, came to let him in.

His parents had to find out what was going on, of course, and when they did, Roddy wasn't sure that he wouldn't rather have had their disapproval.

"He could be doing a good deal worse with his time," his mother said to his father. "I've heard about those model

33

ships that old Mr Nixon makes. And do you know, people'll pay him as much as fifty pounds for one. I'd like to see our Roddy taking up a hobby like that."

"I wouldn't mind giving him a bit of help if that's what he wants," his father said. "I could fit up a work-bench at the end of the garage, easy. He'd have to pay for some of the tools himself, though. Tools cost money, you know. You don't get them for nothing."

They tried to persuade him. It wouldn't cost much. His dad would help him. If he would pay five pounds of his savings his dad would find another five.

But it just made him angry when they talked. "How can I pay five pounds for anything?" he shouted at them. "I'm saving up for my guitar, aren't I?"

They didn't understand. Parents never understood anything. He didn't want a work-bench at the end of the garage. What he wanted was to be able to go to all those places that Mr Nixon talked about. Places with names like Walvis Bay and Galveston and Wanganui. It'd make Mr Nixon die of laughing if he knew that the only place he'd been to outside London was to Clacton on the bus. It would be different when he left school, though. All he had to do was to get his guitar and learn to play it properly. Groups like the Rascals travelled everywhere, to New York, and Japan, and all over.

And then, on the very last Friday of the holidays, it happened. Lying in bed that night he heard the bells of the fire-engines coming, and then going by, and on up towards the main road. He had forgotten it by the morning, but at breakfast-time his mother had somehow got hold of the news. Mr Nixon's shop had been burnt out the night before.

"The fire started in the work-room at the back, so they say," she told him. "He's been taken to hospital, but I don't think he's hurt very bad. Mostly shock, I expect; an old man like that."

He didn't say anything at all. After breakfast he went up to the shop as usual. There was nothing there except a black hole between the houses on either side. He wondered

34

what had happened to all the ~~door~~-knobs and water-taps. There was nothing left at all of the shop or of the work-room either. All that he was able to recognize, under the blackened bricks and bits of charred wood, was something that might have been that old brass bedstead. All the pictures of ships on the work-room walls had gone, and the bench, and the cigar-boxes, and the almost finished model of the *Margaret Macann*.

He walked about the streets for a long while. He didn't know what to do. He thought he might go to the Science Museum. Or perhaps he would take his boat down to the pond. But in the end he walked all the way to Paddington, past the railway station, to the big hospital where his mother had said Mr Nixon had been taken.

The courtyard of the hospital was full of kids, and teenagers too, mostly girls. A porter was trying to tell them to stop making such a row.

"This is a hospital," the porter kept on saying. "If you don't quieten down a bit I'll have the police-dog handlers here to chase you all out of it."

Roddy asked one of the kids what was happening, and the kid told him that Colin Connolly of the Rascals was inside and they were all waiting for him to come out. The porter was standing in the door, not letting any of the kids get near, but Roddy went up to him and said that he had come to see a friend who was ill inside. So the porter let him in and told him to go to the desk where it said 'Inquiries'.

There was another porter at the desk. Roddy had to answer a lot of questions. They wanted to know if Mr Nixon was a relative so Roddy said yes he was. "He's my uncle," he added.

After that they told him to go up in the lift to the third floor. When he got out of the lift he could see through into a long room with beds on both sides, but a nurse wouldn't let him go in.

"You'll have to wait a little," she told him. "You can sit down on the bench over there."

There was already someone else sitting on the bench, waiting. It was Colin Connolly.

Roddy sat right at the end of the bench. He kept on looking at Colin Connolly, but every time Colin caught him at it he looked quickly away. After a little while Colin said to him, "You waiting to see someone then? Who is it, your dad?"

He spoke in strong Mersey, in what they called scouse, just like Mr Nixon. Roddy wasn't able to speak but he shook his head at the question.

"I'm waiting to see my granda'," Colin went on. "He got hurt in a fire last night."

At first Roddy thought that there must have been two fires, but then a nurse came up and said, "You are both waiting to see Mr Nixon, aren't you? I am afraid you will have to wait a little while longer."

Colin Connolly stared in astonishment. "What, are you waiting to see my old granda' too. Is he a friend of yours, then?"

Soon after that Roddy found himself talking away to Colin Connolly just as if he weren't one of the Rascals at all. He told him about the pond in the park and how he had met the old man, and all about the work-shop and the model ships and everything.

"Ah," Colin Connolly nodded. "He's a great one for model ships, my old granda'. Don't suppose he'll make many more, though. They tell me he got his hands burned pretty bad."

"Oh, but he must," cried Roddy. "What about the *Margaret Macann?*"

"What about the who?" Colin Connolly demanded.

"That's the one he's been working on for years. She was the first ship he ever sailed on, years ago."

Colin shot a sideways look at Roddy that was exactly like one of those looks of the old man's. Then be grinned.

"He's been filling you up with that stuff, eh? All about getting wrecked off St David's Head and that, I bet."

"Why... why, wasn't he wrecked, then?" Roddy asked.

That made Colin laugh so loudly that the nurse looked up from her desk and ssshed him with a frown.

"How could he ever get wrecked then, seeing as the

farthest he ever sailed from the Pool was the other side of the Mersey on the Birkenhead ferry?"

"But..." Roddy gulped. "It's not true. He's been everywhere. He told me. To... to New Zealand and... and Honolulu and everywhere."

Colin laughed again, though not so loudly. "I tell you, kid... I ought to know—he's my granda', ain't he? He's dead scared of the sea. You wouldn't get him on a ship if you paid him a pension."

Roddy jumped up. "You're a liar. You're just a rotten liar, that's all you are...."

The nurse was on her feet, too. "Now really," she said, "if you don't keep quiet I shan't let you wait."

But Roddy had already turned his back and was running for the stairs.

Outside the crowd of kids and teenagers were still waiting.

"Hey! Is Colin Connolly still in there?" they wanted to know.

But he pushed by, without saying anything, towards the gates.

When he got home his dad was back from work and had eaten his dinner. They didn't grumble at him for being late.

"I'll tell you what," his father said. "If you like, when you've had your dinner, I'll walk up to the hospital with you to see how old Mr Nixon is getting on."

But what his mother said, as he ran out into the hall and up the stairs to his own room, was, "Well, good gracious! Did you notice? He's been and had his hair cut."

Adolf

D. H. Lawrence

When we were children our father often worked on the night-shift. Once it was spring-time, and he used to arrive home, black and tired, just as we were downstairs in our nightdresses. Then night met morning face to face, and the contact was not always happy. Perhaps it was painful to my father to see us gaily entering upon the day into which he dragged himself soiled and weary. He didn't like going to bed in the spring morning sunshine.

But sometimes he was happy, because of his long walk through the dewy fields in the first daybreak. He loved the open morning, the crystal and the space, after a night down pit. He watched every bird, every stir in the trembling grass, answered the whinnying of the peewits, and tweeted to the wrens. If he could, he also would have whinnied and tweeted and whistled in a native language that wasn't human. He liked non-human things best.

One sunny morning we were all sitting at table when we heard his heavy slurring walk up the entry. We became uneasy. His was always a disturbing presence, trammelling. He passed the window darkly, and we heard him go into the scullery and put down his tin bottle. But directly he came into the kitchen we felt at once that he had something to communicate. No one spoke. We watched his black face for a second.

"Give me a drink," he said.

My mother hastily poured out his tea. He went to pour it out into his saucer. But instead of drinking it he suddenly put something on the table among the tea-cups. A tiny brown rabbit! A small rabbit, a mere morsel, sitting against the bread as still as if it were a made thing.

"A rabbit! a young one! Who gave it to you, Father?"

But he laughed, enigmatically, with a sliding motion of

his yellow-gray eyes, and went to take off his coat. We pounced on the rabbit.

"Is it alive? Can you feel its heartbeat?"

My father came back and sat down heavily in his arm-chair. He dragged his saucer to him, and blew his tea, pushing out his red lips under his black moustache.

"Where did you get it, Father?"

"I picked it up," he said, wiping his fore-arm over his mouth and beard.

"Where?"

"It's a wild one!" came my mother's quick voice.

"Yes, it is."

"Then why did you bring it?" cried my mother.

"Oh, we wanted it," came our cry.

"Yes, I've no doubt you did," retorted my mother. But she was drowned in our clamour of questions. On the field-path my father had found a dead mother rabbit and three dead little ones—this one alive, but unmoving.

"But what had killed them, Daddy?"

"I couldn't say, my child. I s'd think she'd aten some-thing."

"Why did you bring it!" again my mother's voice of condemnation. "You know what it will be."

My father made no answer, but we were loud in protest.

"He must bring it. It's not big enough to live by itself."

"It would die," we shouted.

"Yes, and it will die now. And then there'll be another outcry."

My mother set her face against the tragedy of dead pets. Our hearts sank.

"It won't die, Father, will it? Why will it? It won't."

"I s'd think not," said my father.

"You know well enough it will. Haven't we had it all before!" said my mother.

"They dunna always pine," replied my father testily.

But my mother reminded him of other little wild animals he had brought, which had sulked and refused to live, and brought storms of tears and trouble in our house of lunatics. Trouble fell on us. The little rabbit sat on our

39

lap, unmoving, its eyes wide and dark. We brought it milk, warm milk, and held it to its nose. It sat as still as if it was far away, retreated down some deep burrow, hidden, oblivious. We wetted its mouth and whiskers with drops of milk. It gave no sign, did not even shake off the wet, white drops. Somebody began to shed a few secret tears.

"What did I say?" cried my mother. "Take it and put it down in the field."

So I passed the order to my sister and mother. The rabbit was not to be spoken to, or even looked at. Wrapping it in a piece of flannel, I put it in an obscure corner of the cold parlour, and put a saucer of milk before its nose. My mother was forbidden to enter the parlour while we were at school.

"As if I should take any notice of your nonsense," she cried, affronted. Yet I doubt if she ventured into the parlour.

At midday, after school, creeping into the front room, there we saw the rabbit still and unmoving in the piece of flannel. Strange grey-brown neutralization of life, still living! It was a sore problem to us.

"Why won't it drink its milk, Mother?" we whispered. Our father was asleep.

"It prefers to sulk its life away, silly little thing."

A profound problem. Prefers to sulk its life away! We put young dandelion leaves to its nose. The sphinx was not more oblivious. Yet its eye was bright.

At teatime, however, it had hopped a few inches, out of its flannel, and there it sat again, uncovered, a little solid cloud of muteness, with unmoving whiskers. Only its side palpitated slightly with life.

Darkness came. My father set out for work. The rabbit was still unmoving. Dumb despair was coming over the sisters, a threat of tears before bedtime. Clouds of my mother's anger gathered as she muttered against my father's wantonness.

Once more the rabbit was wrapped in the old pit-singlet. But now it was carried into the scullery and put under the copper fireplace, that it might imagine itself inside a burrow. The saucers were placed about, four or five, here and there on the floor, so that if the little creature should chance to hop abroad it could not fail to come upon some food. After this my mother was allowed to take from the scullery what she wanted and then she was forbidden to open the door.

When morning came and it was light, I went downstairs. Opening the scullery door, I heard a slight scuffle. Then I saw dabbles of milk all over the floor and tiny rabbit-droppings in the saucers. And there was the miscreant, the tips of his ears showing behind a pair of boots. I peeped at him. He sat bright-eyed and askance, twitching his nose and looking at me while not looking at me.

He was alive—very much alive. But we were still afraid to trespass much on his confidence.

"Father!" My father was arrested at the door. "Father, the rabbit's alive!"

"Back your life it is," said my father.

"Mind how you go in."

By evening, however, the little creature was tame, quite tame. He was christened Adolf. We were enchanted by him. We couldn't really love him, because he was wild and loveless to the end. But he was an unmixed delight.

We decided he was too small to live in a hutch—he must live at large in the house. My mother protested, but in vain. He was so tiny. So we had him upstairs, and he dropped tiny pills on the bed, and we were enchanted.

Adolf made himself instantly at home. He had the run of the house and was perfectly happy, with his tunnels and his holes behind the furniture.

We loved him to take meals with us. He would sit on the table humping his back, sipping his milk, shaking his whiskers and his tender ears, hopping off and hobbling back to his saucer, with an air of supreme unconcern. Suddenly he was alert. He hobbled a few tiny paces, and reared himself up inquisitively at the sugar-basin. He fluttered his tiny forepaws, and then reached and laid them on the edge of the basin, whilst he craned his thin neck and peeped in. He trembled his whiskers at the sugar, then did

41

his best to lift down a lump.

"*Do* you think I will have it! Animals in the sugar-pot!" cried my mother with a rap of her hand on the table.

Which so delighted the electric Adolf that he flung his hindquarters and knocked over a cup.

"It's your own fault, Mother. If you left him alone—"

He continued to take tea with us. He rather liked warm tea. And he loved sugar. Having nibbled a lump, he would turn to the butter. There he was shoo'd off by our parent. He soon learned to treat her shooing with indifference. Still, she hated him to put his nose in the food. And he loved to do it. And one day between them they overturned the cream-jug. Adolf deluged his little chest, bounced back in terror, was seized by his little ears by my mother and bounced down on the hearth-rug. There he shivered in momentary discomfort, and suddenly set off in a wild flight to the parlour.

This last was his happy hunting-ground. He had cultivated the bad habit of pensively nibbling certain bits of cloth in the hearthrug. When chased from this pasture, he would retreat under the sofa. There he would twinkle in meditation until suddenly, no one knew why, he would go off like an alarm clock. With a sudden bumping scuffle he would whirl out of the room, going through the doorway with his little ears flying. Then we would hear his thunderbolt hurtling in the parlour, but before we could follow, the wild streak of Adolf would flash past us, on an electric wind that swept him round the scullery and carried him back, a little mad thing, flying possessed like a ball round the parlour. After which ebullition he would sit in a corner composed and distant, twitching his whiskers in abstract meditation. And it was in vain we questioned him about his outbursts. He just went off like a gun, and was as calm after it as a gun that smokes placidly.

Alas! he grew up rapidly. It was almost impossible to keep him from the outer door.

One day, as we were playing by the stile, I saw his brown shadow loiter across the road and pass into the field that faced the houses. Instantly a cry of 'Adolf!'—a cry he knew full well. And instantly a wind swept him away down the sloping meadow, tail twinkling and zig-zagging through the grass. After him we pelted. It was a strange sight to see him, ears back, his little loins so powerful, flinging the world behind him. We ran ourselves out of breath, but we could not catch him. Then somebody headed him off, and he sat with sudden unconcern, twitching his nose under a bunch of nettles.

His wanderings cost him a shock. One Sunday morning my father had just been quarrelling with a pedlar, and we were hearing the aftermath indoors, when there came a sudden unearthly scream from the yard. We flew out; there sat Adolf cowering under a bench, whilst a great black-and-white cat glowered intently at him a few yards away. Sight not to be forgotten. Adolf rolling back his eyes and parting his strange muzzle in another scream, the cat stretching forward in slow elongation.

Ha! how we hated that cat! How we pursued him over the chapel wall and across the neighbours' gardens. Adolf was still only half-grown.

"Cats!" said my mother. "Hideous detestable animals! Why do people harbour them?"

But Adolf was becoming too much for her. Suddenly to hear him clumping downstairs when she was alone in the house was startling. And to keep him from the door impossible. Cats prowled outside. It was worse than having a child to look after. Yet we would not have him shut up. He became more lusty, more callous than ever. He was a strong kicker, and many a scratch on face and arms did we owe to him. But he brought his own doom on himself. The lace curtains in the parlour—my mother was rather proud of them—fell on the floor very full. One of Adolf's joys was to scuffle wildly through them as though through some foamy undergrowth. He had already torn rents in them.

One day he entangled himself altogether. He kicked, he whirled round in a mad nebulous inferno. He screamed—and brought down the curtain-rod with a smash, right on the best beloved geranium just as my mother rushed in. She extricated him, but she never forgave him.

Even we understood that he must go. It was decided, after a long deliberation, that my father should carry him back to the wild woods. Once again he was stowed into the great pocket of the pit-jacket.

"Best pop him i' the' pot," said my father, who enjoyed raising the wind of indignation.

And so, next day, our father said that Adolf, set down on the edge of the coppice, had hopped away with utmost indifference, neither elated nor moved. We heard it and believed. But many, many were the heart-searchings. How would the other rabbits receive him? Would they smell his tameness, his humanized degradation, and rend him? My mother pooh-poohed the extravagant idea.

However, he was gone, and we were rather relieved. My father kept an eye open for him. He declared that several times, passing the coppice in the early morning, he had seen Adolf peeping through the nettle-stalks. He had called him in an odd, high-voiced, cajoling fashion. But Adolf had not responded. Wildness gains so soon upon its creatures. And they become so contemptuous then of our tame presence. So it seemed to me. I myself would go to the edge of the coppice, and call softly. I myself would imagine bright eyes between the nettle-stalks, flash of a white scornful tail past the bracken. That insolent white tail, as Adolf turned his flank on us.

One of the Virtues

Stan Barstow

The watch belonged to my grandfather, and it hung on a hook by the head of his bed where he had lain for many long weeks. The face was marked off in Roman numerals, the most elegant figures I had ever seen. The case was of gold, heavy and beautifully chased; and the chain was of gold too, and wonderfully rich and smooth in the hand. The mechanism, when you held the watch to your ear, gave such a deep, steady ticking that you could not imagine its ever going wrong. It was altogether a most magnificent watch, and when I sat with my grandfather in the late afternoon, after school, I could not keep my eyes away from it, dreaming that someday I too might own such a watch.

It was almost a ritual for me to sit with my grandfather for a little while after tea. My mother said he was old and drawing near his time, and it seemed to me that he must be an incredible age. He liked me to read to him from the evening paper while he lay there, his long hands, soft and white now from disuse and fined down to skin and bone by illness and age, fluttered restlessly about over the sheets, like a blind man reading braille. He had never been much of a reader himself and it was too much of an effort for him now. Possibly because he had had so little education, no one believed in it more, and he was always eager for news of my progress at school. The day I brought home the news of my success in the County Minor Scholarship examination he sent out for half an ounce of twist and found the strength to sit up in bed for a smoke.

"Grammar School next, then, Will?" he said, pleased as Punch.

"Then college," I said, seeing the path straight before me.

"Then I shall be a doctor."

"Aye, that he will, I've no doubt," my grandfather said.

"But he'll need plenty o' patience afore that day. Patience an' hard work, Will lad."

Though, as I have said, he had little book-learning, I thought sometimes as I sat with my grandfather that he must be one of the wisest men in Yorkshire; and these two qualities—patience and the ability to work hard—were the cornerstones of his philosophy of life.

"Yes, Grandad," I told him. "I can wait."

"Aye, Will, that's t'way to do it. That's t'way to get on, lad."

The smoke was irritating his throat, and he laid aside the pipe with a sigh that seemed to me to contain regret for all the bygone pleasures of a lifetime, and he fidgeted with the sheets. "It must be gettin' on, Will...."

I took down the watch and gave it to him. He gazed at it for some moments, winding it up a few turns. When he passed it back to me I held it, feeling the weight of it.

"I reckon he'll be after a watch like that hisself, one day, eh, Will?"

I smiled shyly, for I had not meant to covet the watch so openly. "Someday, Grandad," I said. I could never *really* imagine the day such a watch could be mine.

"That watch wa' gi'n me for fifty year o' service wi' my firm," my grandfather said. " 'A token of appreciation,' they said... It's theer, in t'back, for you to see...."

I opened the back and looked at the inscription there: 'For loyal service....'

Fifty years... My grandfather had been a blacksmith. It was hard now to believe that these pale, almost transparent hands had held the giants tongs or directed the hammer in its mighty downward swing. Fifty years... Five times my own age. And the watch, prize of hard work and loyalty, hung, proudly cherished, at the head of the bed in which he was resting out his days. I think my grandfather spoke to me as he did partly because of the great difference in our ages and partly because of my father. My mother never spoke of my father, and it was my grandfather who cut away some of the mystery with which my mother's silence had shrouded him. My father, Grandfather told me, had been a promising young man cursed with a weakness. Impatience was his weakness: he was impatient to make money, to be a success, to impress his friends; and he lacked the perseverance to approach success steadily. One after the other he abandoned his projects, and he and my mother were often unsure of their next meal. Then at last, while I was still learning to walk, my father, reviling the lack of opportunity in the mother country, set off for the other side of the world and was never heard of again. All this my grandfather told me, not with bitterness or anger, for I gathered he had liked my father, but with sorrow that a good man should have gone astray for want of what, to my grandfather, was a simple virtue, and brought such a hard life to my mother, Grandfather's daughter.

So my grandfather drifted to the end; and remembering those restless fingers I believe he came as near to losing his patience then as at any time in his long life.

One evening at the height of summer, as I prepared to leave him for the night, he put out his hand and touched mine. "Thank y', lad," he said in a voice grown very tired and weak. "An' he'll not forget what I've told him?"

I was suddenly very moved; a lump came into my throat. "No, Grandad," I told him, "I'll not forget."

He gently patted my hand, then looked away and closed his eyes. The next morning my mother told me that he had died in his sleep.

They laid him out in the damp mustiness of his own front room, among the tasselled chairback covers and the lustres under their thin glass domes; and they let me see him for a moment. I did not stay long with him. He looked little different from the scores of times I had seen him during his illness, except that his fretting hands were stilled beneath the sheet, and his hair and moustache had the inhuman antiseptic cleanliness of death. Afterwards, in the quiet of my own room, I cried a little, remembering that I should see him no more, and that I had talked with him and read to him for the last time.

After the funeral the family descended upon us in force for the reading of the will. There was not much to quarrel

47

about: my grandfather had never made much money, and what little he left had been saved slowly, thriftily over the years. It was divided fairly evenly along with the value of the house, the only condition being that the house was not to be sold, but that my mother was to be allowed to live in it and take part of her livelihood from Grandfather's smallholding (which she had in fact managed during his illness) for as long as she liked, or until she married again, which was not likely, since no one knew whether my father was alive or dead.

It was when they reached the personal effects that we got a surprise, for my grandfather had left his watch to me! "Why your Will?" my Uncle Henry asked in surly tones. "I've two lads o' me own and both older than Will."

"An' neither of 'em ever seemed to know their grandfather was poorly," my mother retorted, sharp as a knife.

"Young an' old don't mix," Uncle Henry muttered, and my mother, thoroughly ruffled, snapped back, "Well, Will an' his grandfather mixed very nicely, and your father was right glad of his company when there wasn't so much of anybody else's."

This shot got home on Uncle Henry, who had been a poor sick-visitor. It never took my family long to work up a row and listening from the kitchen through the partly open door, I waited for some real north-country family sparring. But my Uncle John, Grandfather's eldest son, and a fair man, chipped in and put a stop to it. "Now that's enough," he rumbled in his deep voice. "We'll have no wrangling' wi' the old man hardly in his coffin." There was a short pause, and I could imagine him looking round at everyone. "I'd a fancy for that watch meself, but me father knew what he was about an' if he chose to leave it young Will, then I'm not goin' to argue about it." And that was the end of it; the watch was mine.

The house seemed very strange without my grandfather and during the half-hour after tea, when it had been my custom to sit with him, I felt for a long time greatly at a loss. The watch had a lot to do with this feeling. I still admired it in the late afternoon but now it hung by the mantleshelf in the kitchen where I had persuaded my mother to let it be. My grandfather and his watch had always been inseparable in my mind, and to see the watch without at the same time seeing him was to feel keenly the awful finality of his going. The new position of the watch was in the nature of a compromise between my mother and me. While it was officially mine, it was being held in trust by my mother until she considered me old enough and careful enough to look after it. She was all for putting it away till that time, but I protested so strongly that she finally agreed to keep it in the kitchen where I could see it all the time, taking care, however, to have it away in a drawer when any of the family were expected, because, she said, there was no point in 'rubbing it in.'

The holidays came to an end and it was time for me to start my first term at the Grammar School in Cressley. A host of new excitements came to fill my days. I was cast into the melting pot of the first form and I had to work for my position in that new fraternity along with twenty-odd other boys from all parts of the town. Friendships were made in those first weeks which would last into adult life. One formed first opinions about one's fellows, and one had one's own label stuck on according to the first impression made. For first impressions seemed vital, and it looked as though the boy who was lucky or clever enough to assert himself favourably at the start would have an advantage for the rest of his schooldays.

There are many ways in which a boy—or a man—may try to establish himself with his fellows. One or two of my classmates grovelled at everyone's feet, while others took the opposite line and tried systematically to beat the form into submission, starting with the smallest boy and working up till they met their match. Others charmed everyone by their skill at sports, and others by simply being themselves and seeming hardly to make any effort at all. I have never made friends easily and I was soon branded as aloof. For a time I did little more than get on speaking terms with my fellows.

One of our number was the youngest son of a well-to-do

local tradesman, and he had a brother who was a prefect in the sixth. His way of asserting himself was to parade his possessions before our envious eyes; and while these tactics did not win him popularity they gained him a certain following and made him one of the most discussed members of the form. Crawley's bicycle was brand new and had a three-speed gear, an oil-bath gearcase, a speedometer, and other desirable refinements. Crawley's fountain pen matched his propelling pencil and had a gold nib. His football boots were of the best hide, and his gym slippers were reinforced with rubber across the toes. Everything, in fact, that Crawley had was better than ours. Until be brought the watch.

He flashed it on his wrist with arrogant pride, making a great show of looking at the time. His eldest brother had brought it from abroad. He'd even smuggled it through the customs especially for him. Oh, yes, said Crawley, it had a sweep second-hand and luminous figures, and wasn't it absolutely the finest watch we had ever seen? But I was thinking of my grandfather's watch: *my* watch now. There had never been a watch to compare with that. With heart-thumping excitement I found myself cutting in on Crawley's self-satisfied eulogy.

"I've seen a better watch than that."

"Gerraway!"

"Yes I have," I insisted. "It was my grandfather's. He left it to me when he died."

"Well show us it," Crawley said.

"I haven't got it here."

"You haven't got it at all," Crawley said. "You can't show us it to prove it."

I could have knocked the sneer from his hateful face in rage that he could doubt the worth of the watch for which my grandfather had worked fifty years.

"I'll bring it this afternoon," I said, "then you'll see!"

The hand of friendship was extended tentatively in my direction several times that morning. I should not be alone in my pleasure at seeing Crawley taken down a peg. As the clock moved with maddening slowness to half-past twelve

50

I thought with grim glee of how in one move I would settle Crawley's boasting and assert myself with my fellows. On the bus going home, however, I began to wonder how on earth I was going to persuade my mother to let me take the watch out of doors. But I had forgotten that today was Monday, washing day, when my mother put my grandfather's watch in a drawer, away from the steam. I had only to wait for her to step outside for a moment, and I could slip the watch into my pocket. She would not miss it before I came home for tea. And if she did, it would be too late.

I was too eager and excited to wait for the return bus, and after dinner I got my bike out of the shed. My mother watched me from the kitchen doorway and I could imagine her keen eyes piercing the cloth of my blazer to where the watch rested guiltily in my pocket.

"Are you going on your bike, then, Will?"

I said, "Yes, Mother," and feeling uncomfortable under that direct gaze, began to wheel the bike across the yard.

"I thought you said it needed mending or something before you ride it again...?"

"It's only a little thing," I told her. "It'll be all right."

I waved goodbye and pedalled out into the street while she watched me, a little doubtfully, I thought. Once out of sight of the house I put all my strength on the pedals and rode like the wind. My grandfather's house was in one of the older parts of the town, and my way led through a maze of steep cobbled streets between long rows of houses. I kept up my speed, excitement coursing through me as I thought of the watch and revelled in my hatred of Crawley. Then from an entry between two terraces of houses a mongrel puppy darted into the street. I pulled at my back brake. The cable snapped with a click—that was what I had intended to fix. I jammed on the front brake with the puppy cowering foolishly in my path. The bike jarred to a standstill, the back end swinging as though catapulted over the pivot of the stationary front wheel, and I went over the handlebars.

A man picked me up out of the gutter. "All right, lad?"

I nodded uncertainly. I seemed unhurt. I rubbed my

51

knees and the side on which I had fallen. I felt the outline of the watch. Sick apprehension overcame me, but I waited till I was round the next corner before dismounting again and putting a trembling hand into my pocket. Then I looked down at what was left of my grandfather's proudest possession. There was a deep bulge in the back of the case. The glass was shattered and the Roman numerals looked crazily at one another across the pierced and distorted face. I put the watch back in my pocket and rode slowly on, my mind numb with misery.

I thought of showing them what was left; but that was no use. I had promised them a prince among watches and no amount of beautiful wreckage would do.

"Where's the watch, Will?" they asked. "Have you brought the watch?"

"My mother wouldn't let me bring it," I lied, moving to my desk, my hand in my pocket clutching the shattered watch.

"His mother wouldn't let him," Crawley jeered. "What a tale!"

(Later, Crawley, I thought. The day will come.)

The others took up his cries. I was branded as a romancer, a fanciful liar. I couldn't blame them after letting them down.

The bell rang for first class and I sat quietly at my desk, waiting for the master to arrive. I opened my books and stared blindly at them as a strange feeling stole over me. It was not the mocking of my classmates—they would tire of that eventually. Nor was it the thought of my mother's anger, terrible though that would be. No, all I could think of—all that possessed my mind—was the old man, my grandfather, lying in his bed after a long life of toil, his hands fretting with the sheets, and his tired breathy voice saying, "Patience, Will, patience."

And I nearly wept, for it was the saddest moment of my young life.

The Magpie

Alan C. Jenkins

If only the bear would come to Rantala. It would be wrong to pray for that, but if only it would come. After all, it had been reported on Radio Finland the other day. Maybe they'd even send a television team to try and film the bear! Erkki had never seen television but he knew they did that sort of thing. He brushed the sweat from his eyes as he wielded the heavy flail and brought it down with a thump on the rye-sheaves spread on the floor of the barn.

The bear! he muttered to himself every time he swung the flail over, taking his turn with the other three threshers. The bear! Thump went a flail. The bear! Over came the swingle. The bear! If only the bear would come to Rantala.

It would be more exciting than a hundred gala days rolled into one if the bear should happen to come that way. The sweat filmed Erkki's eyes but he could see the bear as if it were there, suddenly outside the red-painted Finnish barn where golden orioles plunged past the bean-flowers and Mourning Cloak butterflies basked on the warm rocks.

It would rear up mightily, massively, challenging the men to battle with a defiant snarl. He, Erkki Aaltonen, would rush forward grimly and accept that challenge while the rest were silent in awed admiration. He would give the pelt of the bear, glossy, thick, and handsome, to his mother for a winter-cape and every time folk saw her in it they'd say, "That was Erkki Aaltonen's bear...."

No!—Thump....The bear!—it wouldn't be like that, he knew. If anyone got the bear it should be his brother Vaino. That would be more right. Vaino would slay the bear, coolly and expertly. Vaino was a terrific chap, eight years older than Erkki, knew all about guns and engines and lots of other things. Erkki would like to resemble Vaino

53

when he grew up, pretending that nothing mattered, play it cool, that was what Vaino always said.

Erkki wouldn't mind if Vaino had the glory of slaying the bear—as if it would come! All the same, he could see Vaino standing over the carcase of the bear, his gun smoking, his eyes glinting. That would be splendid. If only the bear would obligingly come so that Vaino could do that.

Watchful for his turn among the quartet of threshers standing round the golden sheaves, Erkki glanced across at his brother and his blood tingled. Vaino was certainly a terrific chap, there was no doubt—

"Watch what you're doing!" cried a flint-hard voice near him and simultaneously he felt a violent jar as his flail clashed with somebody else's. "We've only just got up, and the boy's half asleep already!"

It was Juhani the hired man who spoke. His yellow hair falling across his brow, he glared at Erkki savagely out of his pale eyes—so pale they looked as if they'd been left out in the rain one night and washed clear of any colour. Erkki glared sullenly back, though he was abashed by his lapse. He hated Juhani. He knew Juhani didn't like him—he was always making sarcastic remarks about him at meal-times.

"We've nearly finished this lot," grunted Grandpa Aaltonen, frowning at Erkki. "Then we'll have a smoke. It's hard work swinging a flail, eh, Erkki poika?"

"A bit heavier than scratching with a pen at two and two makes four at the folk-school!" said Juhani, with elaborate sarcasm, and spat on his hands as the threshers prepared to resume their task.

While Juhani was presently bundling up the threshed sheaves with ropes of straw, Erkki went and squatted alongside his brother on the ramp of the barn.

"Vaino," he said in a low voice, diffident of betraying his eagerness. "D'you reckon there's any chance of the bear coming anywhere near here?"

"Sure, maybe he'll borrow a bikini and swim out to the island and say—Hiyah, guys!" Vaino grinned as he uttered the last words in a foreign tongue and an exaggerated twang. Erkki knew Vaino was pretty clever that way—he'd got a stack of American magazines he could read.

"No, I don't mean that, of course. But to the neighbourhood?"

"Could be," Vaino shrugged, breathing out smoke blue and silky into the glittering sunshine. "He was reported twenty miles away in Kivipaa. Maybe he'll thumb a lift this way. Who knows?"

"That bear is a Russian secret weapon, if you ask me," said Grandpa, lowering himself carefully with a sigh of relief.

"Must have come from the forests on the frontier, eh, Gran'pop?" nodded Vaino. He pursed his lips and squinted at the quivering smoke rings he made. "Got disturbed and beetled across into Finland?"

"That's about it," grunted the old man, fishing a little tin out of his overall pocket and beginning to roll a cigarette.

In the distance an outboard engine puttered like a bluebottle on the lake that was hidden by phalanxes of pine trees.

"Who'll that be?" Vaino speculated idly, wrinkling his nose. "Too early for the pastor. He's coming over for the Lyttinen christening this evening."

"Lyttinen having a look at his pike traps maybe," shrugged Grandpa, running the tip of his tongue along the cigarette paper.

While they lounged on the ramp a rustling avalanche behind them suddenly interrupted their desultory talk, as Juhani loosed another set of sheaves from the smoke-stained beams of the barn and spread them over the threshing floor.

"All right, what are we waiting for?" Juhani demanded in his resentful, jagged voice. Erkki stared furiously at the man. You'd think he was the boss instead of simply the hired man. "And if we can all keep time, it'll get done all the quicker."

Erkki ignored his jibe. As he picked up his flail, he

listened to the growing putter of the motorboat which was evidently approaching the little jetty that belonged to the Aaltonen farm. If only the bear would appear in the neighbourhood. If only the motorboat could be bringing a messenger coming to report it. Erkki caught sight of Vaino neatly flipping his cigarette stub out into the yard. The hens scuttled momentarily towards it, thinking it was food. Vaino was pretty good, a really cool chap he always looked! Up and down, up and down impassively, tirelessly, the threshers continued their work which would culminate, literally, in their daily bread. It was all a matter of timing and rhythm, and even the thought of the bear had vanished for the moment from Erkki's mind as he concentrated on the job.

When they had finished threshing all the sheaves that hung overhead in the beams, they would drag out the ancient winnowing machine from under its tarpaulin and separate the precious grain from the chaff....

But they did not get as far as that. Voices could be heard in the distance, from the direction of the jetty. They sounded agitated. Vaino cocked an inquiring eye at Grandpa. The rhythm faltered. As if by mutual consent the threshers strolled to the door of the barn and looked out across the sun-slashed yard where the swallows hawked the insects.

"Sounds like something's wrong?" muttered Grandpa, scratching his chest.

"It's Lyttinen hollering," said Vaino, listening intently. "That's father, too——"

"Bah, it's probably only that Lyttinen fussing," the old man spat impressively into the yard. He turned back to the threshing-floor. "Thinks someone's been raiding his pike-traps."

But as they began to take up their positions again, Olavi Aaltonen, Erkki's father, followed by his Spitz dog Koira, came running into the yard, shouting excitedly. The calves and the hens exploded wildly in all directions. The threshers flung down their flails and crowded out of the barn to meet Olavi.

56

"The bear!" he was mouthing. "Lyttinen has come across from Pyhtahaari. It's killed one of his calves. It's down in the ravine by the old tarmaker's hut. His cousin's keeping watch. He needs help!"

For a moment Erkki hung back from the eager pandemonium, scarcely aware of the shouting and barking. He felt quite queer about it all. A few minutes ago he had been all but praying that the motorboat could be bringing a messenger with news of the bear—and now it had actually happened!

But the odd feeling didn't last long. Erkki was caught up in the general excitement and was also determined not to be left out of the hunt. In case his mother—whom he spied bustling from the house wiping her hands on her red apron and calling out inquiringly—should try to stop him, he slipped off down to the jetty ahead of the men who were conversing in loud, staccato tones as they hurried towards the lake.

Meanwhile, Vaino had run back into the house to fetch his gun—he was the only member of the family to possess one—and Lyttinen shouted impatiently at him, while the outboard engine of the boat puttered fussily.

Cheek by jowl they crowded together in the rocking boat, and Erkki, rather to his annoyance, found himself jammed alongside Juhani the hired man who, for want of any other weapon, had seized a pitchfork. But there was no time to bother about that, everyone was talking about the bear.

"We will give Honeypaw a feast of lead!" cried Vaino, tugging his cap over his eyes and hugging the gun between his knees. He looked a real hunter, thought Erkki, shifting on the thwart in suppressed excitement so that Juhani glanced irritably at him.

"It is lying up in the Black Ravine," Lyttinen shouted above the noise of the engine. "We shall have to smoke it out."

"When I served in the Winter War," said Olavi, "we had a Lapp scout with us. We used to yarn about hunting and the Lapp swore the best part of a bear was the soles of his

57

feet. Delicious, he said they were."

"Give me pig's trotters any day," Vaino quipped and gusted smoke from his nostrils.

Erkki almost hugged himself with incredulous delight. It was all happening as he had wished and prayed. The bear had miraculously strayed into the neighbourhood. There was Vaino sitting on the next thwart, the gun leaning, winking steelily, against his arm....

They were all gay at the prospect of adventure; all except Juhani, Erkki noticed with an inward sneer. He sat silent next to Erkki, holding the pitchfork, tines upward, his yellow hair matted and untidy, his pale blue eyes staring keenly but impassively at duck or grebe that passed across the lake.

"Perhaps he thinks he's Neptune or somebody, with that pitchfork as if it was his trident," Erkki thought contemptuously. He leaned forward and strove to hear what Vaino was saying about hunting. He could see that everybody was listening attentively to Vaino right enough.

Lyttinen ran the boat into a sandy spit of the Phytahaari shore and, clambering out in a jostling crowd, they hauled it up from the water, then made their way into the forest. The dogs—Olavi's and Lyttinen's—partly from relief at getting out of the boat, ran round barking wildly until Juhani struck out at them with the handle of the pitchfork.

Tense with anticipation, breathing as if he had run a mile, Erkki followed anxiously at the heels of the men as they started to climb into the forest, led by Lyttinen who carried his gun like a soldier. Everyone had suddenly become quiet and serious.

Except Vaino. He turned and caught Erkki's eye by chance and winked, then patted his gun with a knowing look.

"Cool cat, eh boy?" he said, talking foreign again. Erkki wasn't quite sure what the expression meant, but he knew Vaino liked using it. It sounded like 'Kuhl ket' and he must try and remember it. Erkki's palms were sweating as he stumbled on through the brooding silence of the forest.

When they had marched a mile, Lyttinen called a halt and explained that they were nearly at the ravine. A little farther on a figure rose so suddenly and quietly out of the undergrowth of blueberries and juniper scrub that Erkki uttered a gasp. For a moment of mingled hope and dread he thought it was the bear.

But it was Alexis Paasakivi, Lyttinen's cousin, a squatly powerful man, with a completely bald head that shone as if it were polished.

They huddled together, conferring in low tones, but they could not keep the excitement out of their voices. None of them had ever dealt with a bear, and they were divided about the tactics to adopt.

They walked to the edge of the ravine and regarded the rocky cleft which Paasakivi indicated. Erkki stared with awe; it was like a dream. Was the bear really there? But the men were too intent to notice him when he spoke.

"That's where he is," said Paasakivi, proprietorially. The ravine ended abruptly in a low cliff, surrounded by rowan trees alight with berries, while the other end broadened out into a sort of corrie thick with stouter growth, among which Erkki could see the ruins of a wooden building, where the old tarworkers had once lived.

"That cleft is not deep," declared Olavi. "Maybe if you fired a shot or two or keep throwing stones, the bear will come out. Eh, Vaino?"

"That is no use," Juhani contradicted, to Erkki's anger. The lines from Juhani's nose to the corners of his mouth were like great brackets designed to prevent unnecessary speech. "We shall have to smoke him out. There is a breeze blowing across the end of the ravine which would carry the smoke to the bear if we move round to the other side."

"We must be careful of the trees," said Paasakivi, for the forest here was his property. "It is dry as tinder."

However, it was agreed that smoking out the bear was the best plan. It was decided that while the men with guns—Vaino, Lyttinen, and Paasakivi—should take up their position some distance along the edge of the ravine, the others, with the dogs, should build a fire as close to the rocks as possible. Once they had succeeded in building an adequate fire they would have to retreat to the top again.

Olavi had brought an axe with which, helped by Juhani and Erkki, he built a sizeable pile of deadwood, some twenty or thirty paces from the head of the ravine. Grandpa found some old hay in the derelict farmstead and brought back an armful of it to start the fire off.

Erkki couldn't help glancing repeatedly at the cleft as he helped, but though he was in a fever of expectation he tried not to show it. He even elaborately made a thumb's up sign to Vaino standing over there with his gun, though Vaino did not see him.

Ranged along the little ravine, Vaino and Lyttinen and Paasakivi sat watchfully, guns ready. Only Vaino had a real hunter's gun, a rifle; the others had shotguns, Erkki saw. Tethered by cord to a fallen tree, the two dogs shivered in anticipation, their hackles erect. They had already caught the scent of the bear and howled and snarled and struggled in a paroxysm of eagerness and fear.

"Don't light the fire yet!" warned Juhani. "Or you will have the forest alight before you know where you are. You want smoke anyway, not flames.

"It will keep the mosquitoes off," said Olavi, smacking his cheek and examining the blood on his hands, "even if it doesn't bolt the bear."

Erkki frowned, he didn't quite know why, but it surprised him how amicable his father was with the hired man.

They covered the pile of fuel with damp moss and green fern and when Olavi—Erkki eagerly gave him a box of matches—put a light to the hay the flames flickered sulkily here and there, seeking a way out. An acrid, belching column of smoke began to roll out, and to Erkki it was like the heady fumes of some diabolic elixir, so exciting was it.

But the men were not pleased, for the breeze had capriciously eddied round and began to drift in their faces.

"The devil ..." Olavi swore. "We have built the fire on

60

the wrong side."

"We must ease it up and maybe the wind will take it," suggested Juhani. With his pitchfork he probed and levered at the bottom of the pile, hoping to influence the fire, but the heat and the smoke made him retreat. Coughing angrily, he moved away and stood leaning on his fork, glowering at the stubborn fire from under his tousled fringe.

"Serve him right," Erkki thought, shifting uneasily as the man looked at him as if he read his thoughts, "for pushing himself forward so much."

"Why don't you send the dogs in?" asked Grandpa, who all this time had been sitting on the fallen tree.

"If we went to the top of the ravine we could perhaps drop rocks on the bear?" Erkki ventured to suggest. Nobody took any notice of him.

"I will try a shot and see if it will rouse him," Paasakivi announced. He was so big he seemed to creak as he stood up. He picked his way carefully along the steep side of the ravine. Stones and earth trickled beneath his feet, and with his free hand he had to steady himself by grasping the blueberry scrub. When he reached a place where he could stand safely, he loosed off one barrel of his gun.

The noise reverberated like cannonfire in the confined space, and Erkki trembled with something like joy. This was terrific. With sparkling eyes he glanced across at Vaino, who stood chewing, the rifle crooked in his arm. But the only result of Paasakivi's shot was a shower of debris from the side of the cliff and the cries of a startled bird. The dogs were beside themselves with excitement now and started to fight so that Grandpa had to kick them apart. In the distance could be heard the desolate bellowing of a cow, probably the heifer whose calf the bear had killed.

Uneasily the men waited, uncertain what to do. Somewhere among the rocks at the head of the ravine the bear was skulking. Meanwhile, even the dogs had grown silent for the time being, abashed by their own frenzy and Grandpa's scolding. The undertone of the fire was the only

61

sound, and a brittle lull had settled on the forest. The sound of a woodpecker several yards away was like the persistent tapping of a hammer.

All at once Erkki felt a breath of wind on his cheek and he saw with a leap of his heart that the blue smoke was drifting towards the rocks. The men had seen it too.

"The wind has gone round again!" Juhani cried. "We must keep the fire going."

While Juhani strenuously ventilated the pile with his pitchfork, Olavi and Erkki brought more fuel. Soon the smoke was rolling so thickly that the cliffside was completely obscured. Uneasily Vaino and Paasakivi and Lyttinen stood up again, guns ready.

Nobody noticed that the cord to which one of the Spitz dogs was tethered had snapped. It was Koira, Olavi's dog. In a shrill, hysterical din, the dog went rushing obliquely across the slope, while its companion yelped jealously. Vainly Grandpa and Olavi shouted to Koira to stop. In a scutter of dust it vanished through the smoke, while Grandpa cursed furiously, feeling responsible that he had not noticed the broken cord in time.

For a while the barking diminished, muffled by the smoke and the rocks. But then the noise burst out again in a renewed clamour. The barking turned to a hideous snarling, but this as quickly changed to a frantic, agonized yelping scream which died away into a whimper which continued long afterwards.

Erkki was almost sick with dismay. He wanted to run and help Koira, but his legs would not move. Besides, things happened too rapidly to think any more about the dog. While the stricken Koira kept up his outcry, through the haze of smoke a ponderous, hulking shape emerged from the rocky cleft. It was the bear, the bear! the realization thumped in Erkki's brain like the flail he had been wielding. The bear! The bear! he had thought, please let it come—and there it was ....

Erkki found that he was not so much surprised at setting eyes on the bear as seeing the speed with which it moved. The bear went padding, swiftly, urgently—nimbly, as if boneless—down the ravine, ignoring the wild shouts of the men running along the chaotic slope.

Then Paasakivi fired and the ravine echoed shatteringly. But he had missed and the bear continued to humple on its way, a shambling, powerful, fat-haunched shape, desperate to escape. Meanwhile, Lyttinen had clambered hurriedly down the slope to get a better shot.

He fired with his single-barrelled gun and Erkki bit his knuckles as he saw the bear stagger. It wheeled round and round in a series of circles; then, snarling horribly, reared up on its hind legs, biting and pawing at a wound in its side.

"Fire! Fire!" somebody was yelling and Erkki saw that Vaino, not fifteen yards above the bear, had raised the rifle to his shoulder. One cool shot and the bear was done for. Vaino couldn't miss. The bear was almost standing still.

"Vaino! Vaino! Get it! Get it!" Erkki found himself shouting, tensing himself for the crack of the rifle. But nothing happened.

"Fire! Fire!" it was Lyttinen who was shouting, fumbling to reload his own gun.

Vaino's trigger clicked, but nothing more. He looked puzzled. Erkki almost stopped breathing. Frantically Vaino rattled the bolt of his gun, tried to fire again.

By now the bear had recovered from its initial shock and, dropping back on all fours, went lumbering swiftly towards the ruined farmstead that stood deep in willow-herb and rowan saplings. Now Vaino had raised his rifle again and this time there was no misfire. The crack of the rifle shot slammed apart the heavy forest air.

But it was obvious that Vaino had missed.

"Honeypaw is not going to take that as a compliment," muttered Grandpa, putting a hand under his overalls to scratch the better.

"You had a sitter!" Paasakivi furiously reproached Vaino. He rubbed his scalp with a handkerchief. Everybody seemed to be sweating. "Why didn't you fire straight away?"

"I tell you it was a misfire," retorted Vaino, his nostrils flaring irritably. "D'you think I did it on purpose? If it comes to that why did Lyttinen not finish the job instead of just tickling the bear? He's going to be ten times more dangerous now."

"I hit him, didn't I?" said Lyttinen. "If you had a reliable gun to back me up with ...."

In spite of their recriminations they spoke in subdued tones as they stood grouped together at the bottom of the ravine, as if afraid the bear might hear them. Spatters of blood stained the trampled blueberry undergrowth and a steady trail showed where the wounded bear had gone. Other than this there was no sign of it, and the huddle of derelict buildings, lapped by a wide swathe of willow-herb in which bumble-bees worked, lay in a silence as foreboding as the ancient, tarred woodwork itself. To Erkki, it seemed like the setting of one of those terrifying legends he used to read when he was a child.

Away on the slope the surviving dog kept up an undertone of yelping, a shrill, spasmodic, keening sort of noise, as if it were aware of Koira's fate. The fire continued to smoulder and the end of the ravine was pencilled with a blue scribbling of smoke.

Nobody knew what to do. Nobody was prepared to venture too near the ruined farmstead. The wounded bear might be lurking anywhere. In the farness of the forest's edge the cow lowed drearily. In the trees the woodpecker went on tapping insistently like someone sending out a zany message in morse. From the lake, invisible below the forest, came the sound of a motorboat. Every sound, it seemed to Erkki, clenching and unclenching his fists, underlined the fundamental, menacing silence. Why didn't Vaino tell the men what to do? Vaino was intent over the action of his rifle, sedulously sliding the bolt in and out.

Olavi Aaltonen was walking slowly towards the rocks to look for his dog that the bear had killed. Erkki started to follow him, but his father sharply told him to stay. Rebuffed, the boy climbed to the top of the ravine again

and walked along the slope above the buildings, through a long bank of wild spiraea which was a froth of creamy blossom. If only someone would act. Erkki's mouth was parched and his hands wouldn't stop sweating. He perched himself on a cluttered mass of storm-felled trees, whose grey, brittle limbs lay half buried in the spiraea and the tindery lichen which covered the floor of the forest.

For some while now the distant motorboat had been silent and presently two men and a boy appeared over the brow of the hill from the direction of the lake. It was the Laakso family. The men had guns; the boy was armed optimistically with a sickle and was wearing a blue and white woollen skull-cap.

The Laaksos and the other men climbed down into the ravine to consult with Paasakivi. Erkki listened eagerly but couldn't hear what Vaino had to say. But at the end of the wrangling the men evidently decided to try shooting at random again, in the hope of flushing the bear or making it betray its whereabouts.

Portentously, Olavi mustered all the men with guns and then, at his signal, a volley of shots rang out, to be echoed sharply and briefly among the trees before the silence of the forest absorbed the din. The only effect of the firing was to bring down a shower of pine-bark splinters from the sagging roofs.

"The devil must have got away to begin with," commented Pietari Laakso, slotting two more cartridges into his gun.

"Not with the wound I gave him," Lyttinen shouted angrily. "He couldn't go a hundred paces."

"You hit him all right?" Pietari asked, and even Paasikivi joined in the protests.

Sitting on the grey tree, Erkki listened intently, for he thought he could hear a kind of snuffling grunt coming from somewhere below him and behind one of the buildings. He dearly wanted to give Vaino the chance of re-establishing himself. Still sitting, he began to edge his way farther out along the fallen tree. A spear of branch impeded him and he had to stand up to get round it.

"Erkki, come back!" shouted Olavi, who had suddenly caught sight of him. "Those trees are soft as touchwood!"

His warning came too late. As Erkki swung himself past the branch, he felt the tree give with a shudder. He tried to scramble back but the whole tangle, which had probably lain there rotting for a score of years, gave way with a rustling crash.

For a moment Erkki was helped by the fact that his shirt had been caught on a branch as he began to fall. He tried violently to fling himself on to the slope. But then the material parted and he was projected head first down the slope towards the buildings. He somersaulted helplessly, while soil and stones and broken branches spattered about him and the tree-tops wheeled overhead.

Bruised, scratched, somehow trying to shout, as if that would have helped him, he went thrashing through a dense patch of willow-herb. As he went slithering against the wall of one of the derelict hovels, he was aware of a violent turbulence near him. Vaguely he saw a huge form rear up, heard a choking, throaty snarl, and knew it was the bear.

Dazed though he was by his fall, he knew he had to act instantly to save himself. As the bear came blundering at him, he rolled away and scrambled to his feet. But he tripped on something, an iron drainpipe hidden by the undergrowth, and stumbled on hands and knees. Sick with fear and expecting at any moment to be crushed by the bear, he staggered up again.

The willow-herb impeded him, almost deliberately, it seemed in his panic. Wildly he thrashed about with his arms, endeavouring to push his way through as if he were trying to swim in some opaque, nightmare sea.

"Vaino! Vaino!" he realized he was shouting and did not recognize his own voice.

Behind him the bear lumbered on, crippled but impelled by its urge to attack the creatures who had wounded it. Erkki dared not look round, but he was aware of the bear's presence by its swift pursuit, the crashing of its body through the tangling foliage, and by the stink of it.

He felt he was drowning in this sea of willow-herb. He stumbled again, ran blindly into an overhanging branch that whipped his face and made him gasp with pain. Somewhere beyond him the air rang with incoherent shouts and suddenly he realized that a figure had come leaping down from above him.

With a sob of breath he turned towards it witlessly, half thinking the bear was attacking from another side. Then he saw that it was Juhani who had jumped or slithered down the side of the ravine. Wielding his pitchfork, Juhani took the bear in the flank. Snarling, its fur matted with blood, the animal hesitated at this fresh onslaught, and Erkki, running on full tilt, arms spread to check himself, knew that he was safe.

Drawing deep, grateful breaths, but still not fully comprehending, he turned to get a glimpse of Juhani defending himself. The man had thrust repeatedly at the bear, but so violently that the tines of the pitchfork stuck in the vast body. Now defenceless, Juhani backed away, while the bear, uttering a series of menacing, tortured gasping sounds, shambled at him.

It had reared up on its hind legs and, to the horrified boy, looked monstrous, a ravening, bloody, furious, terrified wreck of a creature. While he watched, he saw it strike massively at Juhani, saw Juhani stagger, turn, try to run. But the bear was too close. In a thrashing turmoil of stems and leaves, the animal, driven on by the pain of its wounds, blundered upon him.

With a shout of pain, Juhani went down full length, kicked himself clear. But the bear was not to be denied and, with the pitchfork still embedded in its side like a banderilla, savaged him again. Then men, shouting hoarsely, meaninglessly, were pushing their way through the purple sea of willow-herb, jostling Erkki out of their path as they brandished their guns.

A shot rang out, deafeningly close; another. How many shots, Erkki could not have said. The deserted farmstead rang with an overwhelming din of guns and shouts, counterpointed by the barking of the dog on the slope.

Two men had dragged the limp body of Juhani out of the way. The others were still firing wildly at the bear, their hands fumbling as they reloaded. The bear staggered, reeled, as if wondering which way to move. It clawed at the air, incongruously like a man putting up his hands to pray.

The stricken animal seemed to shrink rather than fall. Slowly it sat down on its hunkers, its great head tucked down as if to inspect its shattered body. Then suddenly it toppled over among the trampled willow-herb, whose pink blossoms were pallid in contrast with the blood that was spattered far and wide, even over the boots of the men.

For a long moment the men, only gradually emerging from their frenzy of hate and fear, stood contemplating unbelievingly this caricature of an animal that had strayed into their world. The dog continued to bark. The bumble-bees continued to explore the flowers.

Then somebody ventured to stir the bear with his foot and a gurgling hiccup exploded from it.

"It's dead all right," somebody said, in a hoarse whisper.

"Honeypaw's digesting his feast of lead," Paasakivi said, but his voice was shaky.

Erkki had to clench his jaws to keep back the bitter liquid that surged up in his throat. In his brain the flail thumped regularly, thump! let the bear come! thump! please let the bear come.

They ripped off a door from one of the ruined buildings and, using that as a stretcher, carried Juhani down through the forest, after they had torn up a shirt to bandage his head and arm. When they reached the lake they broke up the door and lashed a couple of planks lengthwise along the thwarts of Lyttinen's boat.

Because of this there was not room enough for everybody, so Erkki had to go in Laakso's boat. He had to sit next to Aukusti Laakso, which irked him, for the boy was four or five years younger than he and chattered interminably about the whole affair as if it was his father who had been in charge of it from beginning to end.

"Great day!" Aukusti kept exclaiming and bounced up and down on the thwart, while Erkki, sick at heart, dully listened to the drone of engines and watched the corrugations rippling out from Lyttinen's boat.

"Great day, Erkki!" Aukusti started up again. "They said you'd've been a goner if it hadn't been for that fellow. Works for your dad, don't he?"

Erkki couldn't even nod, he felt numb at it all.

"Reckon that fellow'll be all right, Dad?" asked Aukusti, swivelling round on the thwart.

"He's tough all right," answered Pietari Laakso, from the stern of the motorboat. "Need a doctor, though. Have to have his head stitched up plenty and his arm's bruk, too."

"You-all shot up that old bear sure enough, didn't you, Dad? Like an old colander he was, full of holes. You could prackly see through him."

Erkki only half heard Aukusti's chatter and the Laaksos' replies. All he heard was the thump of the flail. He'd wished up the bear and then everything had gone wrong. To begin with, when his father came running into the farmyard and yelled out the news of the bear, it was all like a sudden brilliant flash that transformed everything—or as if a curtain had gone up on some marvellous drama.

But after that—everything had gone wrong. Koira—the dog was old, certainly, but he'd been part of the family for as long as Erkki—had been killed. Vaino had ... Erkki frowned, he couldn't understand that ... what had happened to Vaino? ... then Juhani—he owed his life to Juhani probably and he couldn't understand that, either: he and the hired man had always rasped against each other like sandpaper.

When his father shouted and the curtain rose, it was Vaino who should have taken the part of the hero ... shot the bear, instead of missing ... dragged his brother from the jaws of death. And even Erkki's vision of presenting his mother with the thick, rich, glossy pelt—that had gone wrong, too. The bear's fur was thin and faded by the summer sun and now it was riddled, ruined, by shot.

The changed tone of the motorboat engine roused

Erkki from his bitter bewilderment and he saw that they were approaching the jetty at Rantala. Lyttinen's boat was already tied up there and the men were carrying Juhani up into the island. Somebody was running across a field of flax, probably to telephone.

As Pietari Laakso shut off the engine and let the boat cruise in towards the jetty, a magpie rose with a warning rattle from the roof of the boathouse.

"If I had a gun," chattered Aukusti, pretending to swing a gun at the bird, "I'd bring down that old black and white varmint!"

It was a queer thing that, it all happened suddenly, like snapping your finger and thumb.

"Nothing's ever just black and white, you little squirt!" yelled Erkki. Without realizing it he had stood up abruptly in the boat and was watching the magpie, seeing, as if for the first time, its green and bronze-greens and purples and blues glinting subtly as the sun took it. "Can't you see?"

He hadn't meant to say anything like that, the thought hadn't even entered his head. But somehow it had been put into his lips and he knew it was right. He just knew it was right, even though he couldn't have explained. Nothing in life was ever simply black and white. Yet he was as surprised at his own outburst as was Aukusti and for a moment of time the two boys stared at each other, Aukusti open-mouthed and dismayed.

"Why, you're nuts!" Aukusti almost stuttered. "Dad ... he says ...."

"Look ...," Erkki began, speaking through clenched teeth. Then he fell silent. What was the use of arguing? Either you could see or you couldn't. Nothing was just black and white. But even he himself, he had to admit, had until only a few moments ago, failed to realize that.

He frowned wryly, still not completely able to fathom things. Yet he felt strangely satisfied, almost light-hearted, at the sudden revelation. Then the boat bumped against the jetty and without a word to the Laaksos, he scrambled out.

The Bachelor Uncle

Sid Chaplin

To the boy the entire house was an adventure where nothing
could possibly go wrong. His mother and grandmother en-
folded him often, the house all the time, from early rising
until he returned to smooth sheets and the faint fragrance of
lavender. It was only long afterwards that he realized how
much the house depended upon the two women, and the
other one—his grandfather—who rose six hours before the
rest and went soundlessly out to ride at the end of the
dancing rope and return in mid-morning with the coal dust
thick upon his skin and heavy as bee's pollen on his eyelashes.

But at the moment it was the marvellous adventure of
the house—much bigger than the one they had left—with
its succession of rooms. He compared the house in his
mind to a shell, not the dumpy little shells of the hedge-
row snails, but one of the big conch shells that guarded
the top of the rockery; an unfolding spiral of cosy pink
rooms all centred on the kitchen with its prodded mat, steel
fender, and snapping fire. And he had the free run of it all.
After the two-roomed cottage by the river-side it was a
palace. At first he'd missed the busy little tankies which
ran right up the front street, hissing, snorting, and thrusting
the loaded coal wagons with all their might and main. He'd
missed the tankies more than he'd missed the big red-haired
man, the one who'd come in day after day as black as
Grandad. This one had bathed in front of the fire and his
splutterings had been an intrusion. He hadn't liked the way
he said "My back!" or the way his mother responded by
rubbing the flannel over with the flat of her hand, kneeling
beside the man, until the lather was white and clean, then
pouring over the clean warm water until she could use the
towel. They'd laugh together and he'd watch. At those

71

times his mother seemed to forget him. It was like watching through a window but worse because there was no glass.

That hadn't happened for a long time. Not since the day a big red-faced man had knocked at the door. The man had a very quiet voice, and when he carried his mother to the sofa the boy had noticed the brass-buckle of his belt at the middle of his back. Even though he was afraid for his mother he'd wondered why the belt was fastened at the back. And then the women had come flocking in and the big man had taken him by the hand and said, "Come, lad, let's go for a walk."

"Ah want to stay wi' me mother," he whimpered, and fat old Grandma Martin—she was Grandma to everybody in the village—had said, "Now, honey, the nice man'll show ye the river-dogs if ye go quick." So he'd gone, but not before he'd seen the four men with their burden walking unsteadily down the sleepers between the railway lines. Beyond he'd seen the men and lads filing down the gangway with the dead midgie lamps flapping in their jacket lapels.

He knew it wasn't the right time for the men to ride—the buzzer always blew first. "Mister, look!" he said. "Look at all the men."

"Come on, son," said the man. "Else we'll miss the river-dogs."

"But the men—is there no more coal?"

"The pit's idle, Ah reckon," said the man with an uneasy laugh.

"Those men carrying—are they takin' something to *our* house?"

"God help us wi' all these questions," said the big man and wiped his face with a red hankie. "It's only some chaps carrying a part—a part for the tankies," he concluded triumphantly.

"Poor men," said the boy. "No caps."

"It's a hot day, why should they wear caps!" said the big man, and took his hand and hurt him until they reached the tall stems of the blind men's baccy. "Now, quiet," he said. "Them dogs is shy."

They watched and watched but the dogs didn't come out. "Do you believe in river-dogs, Mam?" he said that night. "The big man took me to the river but they didn't come out—he said they smelt us."

But his Mam hadn't said anything. She'd sat in front of the fire and played with the poker. And Grandma Martin had said, "Poor lamb," and his mother had started crying; he'd felt the tears drop on his hands where she held them in her lap. The tears were hot.

A time after Grandma Martin had said, "Come and see your father."

She took him into the bedroom and he looked at the iron bedstead, expecting to see his father. But his father wasn't there. Grandma Martin lifted him up in her arms. "There he is," she said softly. "He's sleeping, so just say goodbye to him."

"Goodbye, Father," he said.

"He'll never wake," said Grandma Martin.

"Did Mam wash his back?" he asked.

"God have mercy," said Grandma Martin and carried him back to the kitchen.

Next to the nice smell of the many rooms the most comforting thing about his grandfather's house was that his mother was his alone; the two old people belonged to him also, entirely. You never looked through glass. The four of us are happy together, he often used to think. There were good days when he watched the men playing quoits, or flew propellers on top of the pit-heap, or made camps at the bottom of the garden. It was good to come out of sleep, all alone in the big bedroom, and see the sun shining through, and listen to the men shouting at the ponies pulling the tubs along the pit-heap. He knew all the noises. The jingle of the screens, the threshing of the big winding engine, the raps that meant away, or stop, or coal, or men hanging on, the hullaballoo of hens at feeding time, or the drowsy murmur of pigeons waiting for the men coming out of the pit to feed them and open the traps.

But the best time was at night.

After tea his grandfather would fill his pipe. "Tell us

about the time ye won the pony race, Grandad." And the
old man would laugh and stroke his moustache, "It wasn't a
proper race, but...." And then would follow the tale he
never tired of, and others, one for every night, until, tired
of the questions, the old man would close his eyes and
say, "Now it's my turn to take a ride again—what's the
hoss's name?"

"Forty winks!" he'd shout. "Forty winks!" And the two
women would smile at each other and at him, and he'd
look at Grandad's magazines or play forts with the fender—
matchsticks for soldiers.

"Ah'll build ye a proper fort," said his Grandad one day.
"Towers, battlements, drawbridge, moat an' all."

And he did. It was a bobby-dazzler and had lead soldiers
and a cannon that shot matchsticks. He'd hold the fort with
the cannon and shoot down the attacking soldiers. 'It's up
to the mark, eh?" said Grandad. And he taught the boy how
to make tanks of bobbins and elastic. There were nights
when the prodded mat was alive with tanks, and shots, and
desperate sorties. But the castle was never taken. It was
impossible to take the castle because it belonged to him and
he was the greatest general that ever was. It was like the
whole house, and the people in it, all his. And didn't his
Grandma say, "He's got ye in the palm of his hand—he'd
sell ye in one street, buy ye in the other!"

"What's the odds," would say the old man with a
pleased grin.

Then one morning there came a different knock at the
door. He went with his mother and was holding her skirt.
He was afraid of the man. He was big and gruff and red-
haired and said, "It's me, Sal—the ship's in for repairs, and
Ah thought Ah'd look up old friends."

"Why, Dan!" said his mother, and her voice was pleased.
"Ye must come in and have a cup o' tea."

His Grandma was pleased too. "Hey, man," she said.
"Who'd have believed it? Went away a bit lad—now look
at him. The model...."

And then her hand went to her mouth.

"And who's this young rascal?" said the man. "Shy is

74

he, my young nevvy?"

He darted behind his mother's skirts. But the man laughed and knelt down beside his mother and put out a big freckled hand. "Ah'll not hurt ye, nipper," he said. "Look what Ah got for ye." It was a trim little ship with a wireless aerial and slanting funnels.

"Doesn't go with my castle," he said sulkily.

The uncle looked at him thoughtfully, then said, "Ah've seen castles by the sea—this ship'll bring provisions and save the soldiers from starvation."

"Look," said his mother, pointing. "The oilcloth can be the sea!" She leaned over the kneeling man. "He's his own ideas," she said. "Don't mind him—he'll be all over ye before the day's out." The man looked up, smiling. She smiled too, and somehow the two smiles became one smile. Once again it was like looking through a window.

"Say thanks to your Uncle Dan," pleaded his mother.

But he moved sulkily away, and the red-haired man said, "Let the lad be—ye don't give presents for thanks ye's!"

Before the red-haired man had arrived he'd made his plans for the morning—he'd play the piano in the parlour, make thunder and lightning and birds singing, then go and watch the pigeons. Now he decided to play with his castle so that he could hear what was going on. Not that he wanted to play with the castle, especially since somebody might mention the ship—but he'd a feeling he must stay, otherwise something awful would happen.

"Are ye staying long?" his Grandma asked the man.

"Ah'm fixed up at the Seaman's Mission," said the red-haired man. "Of course, ye know, Ah've nobody—no relatives—now."

"Why, lad, ye'd be welcome to stay here a day or two," said Grandma. The boy took two soldiers and drove them straight at each other, twisting the bayonets. He was glad nobody noticed.

"Ah could send a telegram..." said the red-haired man. "If Ah wouldn't be puttin' on ye—it isn't as ye're near kin o' mine."

"We're kin right enough," said his mother.

"That's good of ye," said the sailor awkwardly.

"Well, that's that settled," said his Grandma, smiling. "It's quiet here—quiet for a chap that's travelled Ah daresay—but if ye want our company ye're welcome, Ah'm sure."

"It's a lonely life," said the man and looked at his hands as if the solution to a great mystery lay in the great palms and calloused fingers. "Bunks at sea and a bare bedroom in port; and not a soul to call your own."

"And never a girl to welcome the ship?" asked the grandmother.

"Ah was never a one for the lasses," said the red-haired man. His tone was very casual. "Ah reckon me standards are too high... Ah'll be a bachelor all me days." The boy looked up and saw his mother looking at the red-haired man, sadly, as sometimes she looked at him when she put him to bed, but with a kind of half-smile curving her lips. Then the man looked up from his hands, looked at his mother, looked quickly away and said, "Now if... if Ah'd been lucky."

"Ah well," said the old lady, rising. "Some are lucky soon, some late, and only the good Lord knows why...."

She left the room, "Ah've dustin' to do," she threw over her shoulder. "Entertain the lad, Sal. Ye're of an age and there's a lot to tell."

The boy felt the danger again and ran to his mother. "Pet-lamb!" she chided. "Jealous eyes."

"He takes after you more," said the man.

"He's his father's eyes," said his mother.

"Aye," said the man, "Ah noticed that soon as Ah laid eyes on him...." He was silent a moment. "Ye can bear to speak of it... Ah mean, what's past is past, and he was my only brother. Did he say anything before ... he went?"

The boy felt his mother's hand on his head. The mechanical stroking halted briefly, then started again. "It's ten months now," said his mother. "It's no use makin' a habit o' grief. No, he was dead when they brought him out ... there wasn't a mark on him.

"Ah'm glad," said the red-haired man. "Glad he didn't

76

suffer."

"He went out of the house whistling," she said.

"He was a good whistler," said the red-haired man. "He could charm the throstle down from his perch. He was head an' shoulders above me."

"He thought the world of you, ye know," she said. She hesitated. "He always said if anything happened..." Her eyes filled, and the red-haired man leaned forward and awkwardly patted her hand. "Never mind," he said. "Ah shouldn't have brought it up. Let's talk of something else."

And they did. They talked of seafaring and as the red-haired man described strange ports his mother leaned forward with parted lips and intent eyes. They talked of long-ago times, and in the end the two of them were laughing. The talk went on and on, and the old man coming in was so taken up with the visitor that he quite forgot the small, serious boy playing on the mat. But the boy was alert. Winding the tanks or setting up the soldiers his eyes were busy and saw the glow on his mother's face, the little nod his grandparents exchanged. Panic fluttered like a bird inside him as he gravely moved his pieces. He must watch, he must never leave her side.

But it was no use. During the day it was all right, but there was nothing he could do when the red-haired man suggested the pictures or a bit walk down the land. Those nights he lay awake until he heard their footsteps on the pavement outside, the clatter of table-setting, the deep voice saying goodnight—and then he could relax. But not entirely. The small fear was always there. But one day there was a telegram.

The man opened it. "They want you back?" asked his mother.

"Tomorrow," he said shortly. "Ah've a good mind to chuck it...."

"Ye must go to your duty, Dan," she said.

"Sally," he said, "Ah cannot go without sayin'... Ah know maybe it's wrong—but then him and me were only half-brothers. Ah love ye, lass...."

"Ssh!" she said. "Little pitchers have big ears...."

"We'll talk about it tonight," he said. "Tonight for sure."

The boy didn't know what the talking was to be about but felt a danger to himself, all the more because his mother seemed withdrawn. Often he caught her eyes upon him. And that night he was determined not to sleep. He lay awake for centuries and centuries it seemed. He heard his grandparents come to bed, and still the deep voice and the loved voice went on and on. Then there was a long silence.

What he saw when he opened the kitchen door was his mother and the man seated side by side at the fire. The arm of the red-haired man was around his mother. What *they* saw was a small boy with legs like sticks below the flannel nightshirt and the wide frightened eyes. "Mam— Mam!" he cried. "Don't go away from me!" And then they were together, the boy and the mother, and the arm of the red-haired man was withdrawn, and now *he* was looking through the window. The small boy felt a quick surge of joy.

The next morning was overcast and after breakfast it rained. The red-haired man was gone. He had slipped out in the early morning without a word of goodbye; and the grandmother was bustling with assumed cheerfulness.

"Your father was just the same," she said to the boy. "Never could stand a drawn-out parting."

His mother sat with a cold cup of tea in her hand and had nothing to say. The boy arranged his castle but this time the soldiers were on the battlements and the tanks faced outwards. And the beautiful ship was on the oil-cloth with its funnels slanting towards the castle, steaming away to an unknown harbour. He decided to let down the drawbridge now that the battle was over but the little handle wouldn't work so he explored the winder between the two towers expecting to find the minute chains in a tangle. "Look, mother," he said. "Look at all the money!"

And indeed the recess was packed with pound notes, all new and crisp. Suddenly his mother was on her knees beside him. At last she found a piece of paper with writing. His Grandma looked down, strangely still, with the duster hanging from her hand. "What does it say, Sal?"

"He says ...." Her eyes filled. "He says it wouldn't be

78

right." Her eyes were on the boy. "He could never follow on after his stepbrother—the bairn wouldn't...."

"Such stuff and nonsense!" said the old lady. The boy looked down, holding his face from smiling.

And then she wept and her arms went round the boy in a terrible craving for comfort. His grandmother bent to pick up the abandoned money. "Thirty pund," she said in wonderment. "There's all of thirty pund." Her hand passed lightly over their two heads. "Never mind, Sal. Don't grieve, lass; he'll be back some day, you'll see." But the boy, held close to the storm of a sorrow that left his own sturdy craft inviolable, knew better. The bachelor uncle, the intruder, was sailing away never to return, and the house and all its lives would be his alone for ever and ever.

Vanity

Elizabeth Enright

(The Melendy family, made up of Mona, her sister Randy, and Rush and Oliver, their two brothers, were tired of wasting Saturday afternoons because they hadn't got enough pocket money to do anything interesting so they decided to pool their money and take it in turns to spend it—in this way each of them spent one Saturday afternoon in four doing what they particularly wanted. This story is about what Mona did on her Saturday afternoon.)

Randy sat on her bed watching Mona get ready to go. Lunch was over and the dishes washed, but a faint odour of baked potatoes and lamb chops lingered comfortably in the house.

Mona's side of the room was covered with photographs of actors and actresses; some signed and some just cut out of magazines and thumb-tacked to the wall. The most precious ones were framed and stood on her bureau with her brush and comb set, two artificial roses in a vase, and a bottle of perfume called 'Night on the Nile', which had never been opened. It was all very tidy and correct. The only thing about Mona's side of the room which led you to suppose that she wasn't a young lady was her bed. It was very flat (she never used a pillow), and at the head of it sat a giant panda, made out of plush, and an ancient cloth doll named Marilyn whose face had entirely disappeared.

The sunlight came into the room and so did weaving branch shadows from ailanthus trees in the backyard. Mona was brushing her hair; electricity made it stand out in a silken skein, and Randy could hear it crackle like burning leaves. It was almost too bright to look at in the sun. "You have beautiful hair," she said.

"Oh, beautiful!" scoffed Mona, brushing as if she hated it. "Nasty old straight stuff. You and Rush are the lucky ones."

"Rush doesn't think so. He's always trying to make his lie down and be straight. Remember the time he put the

gelatine on it?"

They both laughed. Mona's fingers deftly plaited the golden hair. Then she put on her cleanest sweater and skirt and her green coat and hat that matched. But where were her gloves? She jerked open the bureau drawers, burrowing her way through them till they boiled over. Not a glove in sight. Randy got off her bed and joined the search, and at last they were located in the strangest places! One in the kitchen beside the alarm clock, and one upstairs in the Office on the piano.

"All my gloves behave like that," said Mona, slapping them together as if to punish them. "They never want to stay in pairs."

"They're what the newspapers call incompatible," said Rush. "What are you going to do with your afternoon? Come on, Mona, be a sport." But Mona wouldn't tell. She patted her pocket-book and smiled mysteriously. The truth was she wasn't sure herself.

"Good-bye kids," she said.

Mona walked along the street feeling like the heroine of a play. The whole afternoon lay ahead of her filled with boundless opportunities. It was a cold day, but not too cold. Mona couldn't remember when the air had ever seemed so delicious before. She felt like running, or soaring in great bounding leaps, or shouting noisily. But naturally she did nothing of the kind. She walked sedately along the street, swinging her pocket-book and smiling to herself. She wondered if the people who passed her noticed the smile and thought to themselves, 'Who can she be? What a strange, mysterious smile!' But then (it always happened that way—she caught sight of her reflection in a glass window—and was astonished at how much fatter and shorter she was than she thought of herself as being. Between the swinging braids her round face with its mysterious smile looked perfectly sappy. There was no other word for it. Just sappy.

At Forty-fourth Street Mona pushed the little bell in the railings, climbed over the lap of the stout lady who had sat down beside her, and made a perilous descent to the street.

Across the avenue, then two blocks west, and she was on

81

Broadway! Mona had never been there by herself before, and it was wonderful! For a while she simply drifted with the crowds up one side of the famous thoroughfare and down the other. There was a lot to see and she saw most of it. She studied the pictures in front of the dazzling movie theatre where a doorman in gold braid was bellowing haughtily, "Standing room onlay! Standing room onlay!"

Past Fiftieth Street another window caught her attention. In it there was nothing but a lot of draped pink silk and three wax ladies' heads mounted on stands. Each of the ladies was smiling the same sweet stupid smile, and each was wearing an elaborate wig: one was blonde, one was red, and one, for some reason, was lavender. On the glass in gold letters was written:

Etienne and Edward

Hairdressers and Beauty Specialists

3 items 1 dollar

Mona's heart beat fast, and suddenly she knew what she was going to do. "After all, nobody ever asked me not to," she told herself. "I never promised I wouldn't." But all the time she knew that she was quibbling; the corner of her mind that never let itself be fooled was well aware that neither Father nor Cuffy* would approve of what she was about to do. But nothing could stop her now, and pushing open the heavy glass door she went into the shop.

It was a busy place. People in white uniforms hurried to and fro carrying combs, scissors, bowls of hairpins: every-one was talking. The place smelled of hot hair and perfume. At one side of the room sat a long row of ladies each with her head bowed meekly under a buzzing bell-shaped metal thing.

"Yes, dear?" inquired a voice sweetly.

There was a blonde lady enthroned at a raised desk. She had a round, chalk-white face with nothing in it except eyes, nose, and mouth: no wrinkles, no expression, no smile. It reminded Mona of the Tang goddess from China that Father had in his study at home. Even the lady's hair was like the goddess's head-dress: it was all built up on her head

*Cuffy—the housekeeper and friend of the family

in silvery-golden curls and spirals. It must be done with glue, thought Mona. I don't see how it could stay up that way otherwise, or maybe she uses gelatine like Rush. She had to smile at the thought.

"Yes, dear?" repeated the voice, this time a little more sharply. "Is there something I can do for you?"

Mona flapped her braids nervously. "My hair," she said, "I want it cut off."

The goddess never batted an eyelash. She simply turned her head and called out in a voice like an iron file.

"Oh, Mr Edward," she called, "Oh, Miss Pearl."

Mr Edward was tall and refined looking with wavy dark hair and melancholy eyes like a poet. Miss Pearl was small and pretty with a smile that never left her face for an instant. She talked through it and ate through it, and it was probably still there when she was asleep.

"This little girl would like her hair bobbed," explained the goddess.

"Those lovely braids?" exclaimed Miss Pearl.

"Yes," said Mona firmly. "I loathe them."

"She's quite right too," agreed Mr Edward. He stood away and regarded her through narrow eyes, more like a painter than a poet. "The little lady is definitely the sub-deb type. I see a long bob; about shoulder length. Fluffy. Soft. Youthful." He looked like a man in a trance.

"Well, take her to booth eleven, then, "said the goddess practically. "Etienne's permanent wave just went home a couple of minutes ago, so it's empty."

Booth eleven was hung on three sides with silky green curtains like a little tent. On the fourth side there was a large mirror and a basin all grinning and glittering with faucets and gadgets.

Miss Pearl hung up Mona's hat and coat, draped her with a pink rubber cape, told her to sit down on the important-looking chair in front of the basin and began undoing her braids.

"Such beautiful hair, honey," said Miss Pearl. "Seems like it's almost a shame to cut it off. What'll your mamma say?"

"My mother is dead," said Mona.

"Oh. Oh, well. It sure is lovely hair, though. So long too. Way down to your hips, almost. Are you sure you want to bob it?"

"Absolutely positive," replied Mona.

"Well, okay then. Oh, Mr Ed-ward, "bleated Miss Pearl over her shoulder, and Mr Edward appeared suddenly, dramatically, from behind the curtain, with a flashing smile, like the villain in a play. Iago, thought Mona to herself. He clicked the scissors together, hungrily; then he began. Mona discovered that her heart was beating fast again. Shining strands fell to the floor; into Mona's lap; everywhere. In the mirror she could see her anxious face framed between a long lock on one side and a sort of ragged clump like a cocker-spaniel's ear on the other.

As he worked Mr Edward asked all the usual dull, boring questions that Mona felt she should have out-grown long ago: what is your name, little lady, how old are you, what school do you go to, do you enjoy it, what class do you enjoy most, I bet you enjoy recess most, don't you, have you any brothers and sisters, my, my, isn't that nice, how old are *they*, and what are *their* names, etc.

Goodness, the questions children always had to answer, and politely too. Still he seemed to be a nice man, and Mona had the feeling that he was really just as bored as she was by the questions and only asking them to be kind.

"Oh, dear!" cried Mona in consternation, looking at the horrible reflection of herself in the mirror. She saw a frightened face framed by a lot of straight bushy hair lopped off at the shoulder. "Oh, Mr Edward! I look like an old English thatched cottage. I don't *like* it!"

"Now, now, never mind," he consoled her. "You just wait till we get finished. It won't look anything like this, I promise. Now, let's see-". Mona could tell that he was racking his brains for another question to ask her. Ah, he had it. "And what are you going to do when you grow up, little lady?"

Mona wished he wouldn't call her little lady, but aloud she answered politely. "An actress," she said.

"Well!" said Mr Edward, mildly surprised.

"Isn't that cute!" exclaimed Miss Pearl, to Mona's boundless disgust. "A movie actress?"

"No," said Mona proudly. "A real actress on the stage, like Helen Hayes, or Ethel Barrymore."

"Well, if that's the case we must make you as handsome as we can, mustn't we?" said Mr Edward. "All right, Pearl, you can take over now. Good-bye, Myrna." (Mona saw that he hadn't understood her name.) "Just relax and I'll be back in a flash."

Miss Pearl twirled the chair around and fastened a sort of metal plate to the back of it. At one end of the plate there was a curved dent that looked as though someone had taken a bite out of it.

"Just rest your neck in there, honey," said Miss Pearl. "Now lay your head back, that's right."

Cascades of warm water and foaming suds of perfumed soap flowed over Mona's scalp. Miss Pearl's fingers were light and dexterous. This was something entirely different from Cuffy's brand of shampoo. Cuffy scrubbed as if her hope of salvation depended upon it. When she was through your eyes were red and smarting from all the soap that had got into them, and your whole skull was throbbing as though it had been beaten with a mallet. The Melendy children dreaded shampoo days as they dreaded few things, and Oliver had once been heard begging Cuffy to use the vacuum cleaner on his scalp instead.

Mr Edward wheeled in one of the bell-shaped driers that Mona had noticed in the other room. It grew on a tall stem like a gigantic lily and had a long tendril of wire. Mr Edward adjusted the bell over Mona's head snapped a switch and released a small warm tempest that swarmed suddenly through her hair, and filled her ears with a gentle roaring.

Miss Pearl leaned forward asking a question that Mona couldn't hear. She supposed it was something about whether or not she was comfortable and nodded her head absently. There she sat in her small, windy cave staring at Miss Pearl's long eyelashes against her cheek, and contented smile that curved her lips.

She was so absorbed in these reflections that it came as a frightful shock when Miss Pearl gave her back one of her hands to look at. All five nails had been painted red as blood! Mona was horrified and fascinated at the same time. Cuffy would faint dead away if she ever saw them, but they were so beautiful! Like little red shells, or curved rubies, or even drops of sealing wax, but nothing at all like finger-nails. After all, I can take it off when I get home, Mona told herself. I'll just keep them this way till I get back and look at them once in a while.

"They're perfect," she said, and Miss Pearl's smile was more pleased than ever as she began on the other hand. By and by, when Mona's hair was cooked enough she reached over and switched off the tempest. In the sudden clear stillness Mona could hear the lady in booth twelve telling someone about how she'd eaten something that disagreed with her.

"There we are, honey," Miss Pearl said, wheeling away the drier, and beginning to take the hairpins out.

"I feel like a baked potato," Mona remarked, "and I look a lot like one too."

"Now you just wait, honey," Miss Pearl told her. "You just wait till we get rid of these old pins and Mr Edward combs you out. You won't *know* yourself."

And it was true. Ten minutes later, after Mr Edward had combed and brushed and snipped and fussed over her hair, Mona did not know herself. Great curls and puffs and ringlets frothed above her shoulders and on her forehead. The result exceeded her wildest expectations. She was awed by the beauty of it. Why, I could go into the movies this minute, she thought; only what would Cuffy say?

"Honey, you're a picture!" exclaimed Miss Pearl, clasping her hands in admiration. "I bet you somebody's going to cause quite a sensation when she goes home. I bet her daddy won't know her; he'll be tickled to death!"

Mona had a small pang of misgiving when she thought of Father. Tickled to death wasn't exactly what she expected him to be. But maybe he'd like it when he got used to it.

"Yes, indeed, little lady," Mr Edward was saying. "You

are definitely the sub-deb type. Definitely. Just remember I told you so, Myra."

Mona wasn't exactly sure of what he meant by 'sub-deb type', but she supposed it was a compliment, so she said "thank you" and shook hands with both him and Miss Pearl.

Even the Tang goddess at the desk cracked her mask with a smile.

"You look real cute, dear," she said. "That'll be a dollar fifty."

Well, that took the last penny in Mona's purse, and it was a long way home, but never mind.

All over the city lights were coming on in the purple-blue dusk. The street lights looked delicate and frail, as though they might suddenly float away from their lamp-posts like balloons. Long twirling ribbons of light, red, green, violet, were festooned about the doorways of drug-stores and restaurants, and the famous electric signs of Broadway had come to life with glittering fish, dancing figures, and leaping fountains, all flashing with fire. Every-thing was beautiful. Up in the deepening sky above the city the first stars appeared white and rare as diamonds.

The curls bounced on Mona's shoulders. They blew softly, silkily against her cheek; and inside her gloves she could feel the ten red finger-nails sparkling light-heartedly. It was a long walk home but Mona was carried swiftly on a tide of joy. It's something to discover that you're going to grow up beautiful instead of ugly.

The first person she saw when she got home was Willy Sloper shambling through the front hall on his way to Father's study. Something was probably wrong with the furnace again.

"Hello, miss," he said. "You lookin' for someone? Why—why, *Mona!* What have you been and done to yourself?"

"Don't you like it, Willy?"

"I dunno, Mona. Maybe I do. I ain't sure. I kinda liked them plaits of yours."

Oh well, Willy doesn't know anything, Mona told her-self. All the same she tiptoed up the stairs to the top floor. It was Randy's week to take care of the Office, and Mona

87

was fairly sure of finding her alone.

She was right. Music was pouring out of the radio, and Randy was performing the role of Cinderella in an imaginary ballet. She went leaping and pirouetting around the room flapping the dustcloth along the shelves. Pleasure combined with work whenever possible was Randy's idea. Mona pulled off her hat. "Look at me!" she ordered.

Randy paused in the middle of an arabesque.

"Good night! Why, Jiminy Crickets! Why, gee whiz! Why, Mona! You look wonderful, but how did you ever *dare!* What will Father say? What will *Cuffy* say?"

"Well, it's too late for anybody to say anything," Mona retorted. She was feeling a little scared but it wouldn't do to let Randy know it.

"Look," she said, pulling something out of her pocket. It was the shining bundle of shorn hair. "Marilyn and all the other dolls can have new wigs, and we'll save what's left over to make moustaches for plays!"

Randy's delight was the last pleasant thing about Mona's afternoon: after that everything was horrible. Absolutely horrible. Father could hardly believe that she had done such a thing without consulting him. Cuffy was frankly disgusted, and Rush said, "Jeepers! You look just like everybody. Any of those dumb high school girls that walk along the street screaming and laughing and bumping into people. Why couldn't you have waited a while?"

Oliver was the only one who reacted favourably. He said that she looked exactly like the Blue Fairy in *Pinocchio*, and Mona gave him a grateful hug.

And then the nail polish wouldn't come off. No matter how she scrubbed with soap and water the ten red nails continued to glitter unscathed. She tried cold cream, and cleaning fluid, even peroxide. By the time Cuffy blew two blasts on the police whistle which meant dinner Mona was in a panic. She couldn't eat dinner with her gloves on, and she was too hungry to go without it. She went reluctantly down the stairs with red cheeks and her hands in her pockets.

It was a very difficult meal. Everyone kept looking at her as if she were a stranger; but the red fingernails were what bothered her the most. The left hand could be kept hidden under the napkin in her lap, but the right hand was another matter. She tried holding her fork with all the fingers curved under, which is almost impossible to do, and prayed that nobody would notice. But naturally the prayer was not worthy of an answer.

"Mona!" said Father suddenly. "What on earth is the matter with your hand? Have you hurt it? Open it out and let me see."

Mona opened her hand. The five red nails were bright as stop lights, and she wished that she knew how to faint at will.

"Good Lord!" said Father, and choked on his coffee.

Rush gave a long rude whistle. "Vanity," he said pompously, "thy name sure is woman!"

Randy just looked shocked and kept on eating, and Cuffy made a snapping noise with her tongue against her teeth and shook her head as if she couldn't believe her eyes.

"What in heaven's name has got into you, Mona?" inquired Father, red-faced from choking. "I never thought you were silly or vain. When you're eighteen years old if you want to go in for that sort of thing it will be all right, I suppose. But not now. There's no way we can bring your braids back, but at least we don't have to put up with those talons. I want you to take that red business off your nails immediately after dinner."

"It won't come off," said Mona miserably. "I tried. It has to wear off."

"I'll get it off all right," said Cuffy grimly. "There's plenty of things I can try: gasoline, or sandpaper, or shellac. But I'll get it off!"

Mona bent over her plate. There was such a lump in her throat that she could hardly swallow, and the knives and forks and glasses swam to and fro like fish.

"When are you going to start putting stuff on your face, Mona?" inquired Rush virtuously. "When are you going to start wearing a ring in your nose?"

"Oh, Rush, I hate you!" cried Mona. And she sprang up from the table and fled from the room with a loud

89

undignified sob that came out of her like a hiccup.

Up the stairs she ran blindly. Up to the Office with the door banged behind her, and then face down in the dark on the humpy old couch which received her tenderly. She felt hurt and angry and silly and ashamed all at the same time. There was no comfort anywhere; nothing but the harsh fabric under her cheek that smelled of age and dust.

Out of doors people were walking in the street; Mona could hear their footsteps ringing on the pavement far below. Automobiles containing people whose families loved them hooted by in the winter night. She would simply disappear then, years later, when she came back to New York as a famous actress, they would all (Cuffy and everyone) come to hear, begging forgiveness. And she would be very sweet to them.

Cuffy came into the Office and creaked down on the sofa beside her.

"Go away!" said Mona.

"No, I won't," retorted Cuffy. "You sit up like you had some spine to you."

Mona sat up.

"There's nothing to be breaking your heart about, neither. Everybody does fool things once in a while; I shouldn't be surprised if it was good for 'em." Cuffy was stroking Mona's forehead. Her hand was rough from hard work, and yet it was soft at the same time. Mona sniffed and gulped.

Above the distant noises of the city another sound, high up, purred across the night.

"Listen!" said Cuffy. "Get up, child, and come to the window. Look out."

Every house in the street was bright with windows. A vast luminous glow rose upward from the city, and high overhead against the stars there was a green star that travelled steadily.

"Look up at that," commanded Cuffy. "Nobody, hardly, looks up any more. We hear airplanes without listening to them. We aren't scared of them because they're as much a part of the way we get to places as buses or trolleys or railway trains. They won't harm us; we don't have to be afraid

they'll drop bombs on us. And now look at all them buildings lit up like birthday cakes. There's a town that's never
been touched by a war. It's just as bold and brassy as ever
it was. But what about the cities that were broken by
bombs? Some of 'em aren't mended yet, and I've heard
there's children living like mice amongst the trash and ruins.
And there's other children in the D.P. camps too, plenty of
them. What's nail polish to them. I wonder? What's permanent waves or curls or how they look....? Why, I've heard
that some of them don't know what toys are, even! Right
now there's hundreds of children-"

"Oh, Cuffy, don't!" sobbed Mona." I feel so cheap, I
feel so cheap!" the red nails burned her finger-tips like coals
of fire.

"Well now, well now," said Cuffy, patting her on the
shoulder blades. "It's all right, my lamb. Just quit thinking
you're the hub of the universe, that's all. As for the bobbed
hair, I'm not sure but what I think it's a good idea; we won't
go through such perdition shampooing it from now on, and
the snarls will be scarcer. But them nails! Seems to me like
I read some place perfumery would take it off."

"I have some perfume, Cuffy!" cried Mona, happy to
make a sacrifice. "You wait here."

In a moment she was back with 'Night on the Nile,' the
precious bottle which had never been opened!

"My," gasped Cuffy as the top came off, "sort of blinds
you don't it?"

"I like perfume to be strong," Mona said, sniffing
rapturously. "I like it so strong that people can come into a
room twenty-four hours after you've left, and know that
you've been there."

"Well, this is strong all right," said Cuffy, scrubbing away.
"I bet it would take the veneer right off a piana, let alone
them little nails of yours."

Soon the nails were in their natural state once more, and
both Cuffy and Mona were extremely highly scented.

"I feel like Lillian Russell," remarked Cuffy. "All I need is
a picture hat and diamond bracelets right up to my elbow."

Mona went down to the study to say good night to

Father. The desk was littered with paper and books, and above the confusion stood the little Tang goddess looking serenely into space.

Mona held out her hands with their plain unvarnished nails.

"That's better," said Father, and took one of the hands in his. He sniffed inquiringly.

"We had to use perfume to get it off," Mona explained hastily. "It wasn't because of vanity this time."

Father laughed. "You know, Mona," he said, "maybe I'll get used to that hair of yours when it quiets down a little. Maybe I'll even like it. I suppose parents are always startled when they see their children showing signs of growing up for the first time."

His First Flight

Liam O'Flaherty

The young seagull was alone on his ledge. His two brothers and his sister had already flown away the day before. He had been afraid to fly with them. Somehow when he had taken a little run forward to the brink of the ledge and attempted to flap his wings he became afraid. The great expanse of sea stretched down beneath, and it was such a long way down—miles down. He felt certain that his wings would never support him, so he bent his head and ran away back to the little hole under the ledge where he slept at night. Even when each of his brothers and his little sister, whose wings were far shorter than his own, ran to the brink, flapped their wings, and flew away he failed to muster up courage to take that plunge which appeared to him so desperate. His father and mother had come around calling to him shrilly, upbraiding him, threatening to let him starve on his ledge unless he flew away. But for the life of him he could not move.

That was twenty-four hours ago. Since then nobody had come near him. The day before, all day long, he had watched his parents flying about with his brothers and sister, perfecting them in the art of flight, teaching them how to skim the waves and how to dive for fish. He had, in fact, seen his older brother catch his first herring and devour it, standing on a rock, while his parents circled around raising a proud cackle. And all the morning the whole family had walked about on the big plateau midway down the opposite cliff, taunting him with his cowardice.

The sun was now ascending the sky, blazing warmly on his ledge that faced the south. He felt the heat because he had not eaten since the previous nightfall. Then he had found a dried piece of mackerel's tail at the far end of his ledge. Now there was not a single scrap of food left. He had searched every inch, rooting among the rough, dirt-caked straw nest where he and his brothers and sister had been hatched. He even gnawed at the dried pieces of spotted eggshell. It was like eating part of himself. He had then trotted back and forth from one end of the ledge to the other, his grey body the colour of the cliff, his long grey legs stepping daintily, trying to find some means of reaching his parents without having to fly. But on each side of him the ledge ended in a sheer fall of precipice, with the sea beneath. And between him and his parents there was a deep, wide chasm. Surely he could reach them without flying if he could only move northwards along the cliff face? But then on what could he walk? There was no ledge, and he was not a fly. And above him he could see nothing. The precipice was sheer, and the top of it was perhaps farther away than the sea beneath him.

He stepped slowly out to the brink of the ledge, and, standing on one leg with the other leg hidden under his wing, he closed one eye, then the other, and pretended to be falling asleep. Still they took no notice of him. He saw his two brothers and his sister lying on the plateau dozing, with their heads sunk into their necks. His father was preening the feathers on his white back. Only his mother was looking at him. She was standing on a little high hump on the plateau, her white breast thrust forward. Now and again she tore at a piece of fish that lay at her feet, and then scraped each side of her beak on the rock. The sight of the food maddened him. How he loved to tear food that way, scraping his beak now and again to whet it! He uttered a low cackle. His mother cackled too, and looked over at him.

"Ga, ga, ga," he cried, begging her to bring him over some food. "Gaw-ool-ah," she screamed back derisively. But he kept calling plaintively, and after a minute or so he uttered a joyful scream. His mother had picked up a piece of fish and was flying across to him with it. He leaned out eagerly, tapping the rock with his feet, trying to get nearer to her as she flew across. But when she was just opposite to him, abreast of the ledge, she halted, her legs hanging limp, her wings motionless, the piece of fish in her beak almost within reach of his beak. He waited a moment in surprise, wondering why she did not come nearer, and then, maddened by hunger, he dived at the fish. With a loud scream he fell outwards and downwards into space. His mother had swooped upwards. As he passed beneath her he heard the swish of her wings. Then a monstrous terror seized him and his heart stood still. He could hear nothing. But it only lasted a moment. The next moment he felt his wings spread outwards. The wind rushed against his breast feathers, then under his stomach and against his wings. He could feel the tips of his wings cutting through the air. He was not falling headlong now. He was soaring gradually downwards and outwards. He was no longer afraid. He just felt a bit dizzy. Then he flapped his wings once and he soared upwards. He uttered a joyous scream and flapped them again. He soared higher. He raised his breast and banked against the wind. "Ga, ga, ga. Ga, ga, ga, Gaw-ool-ah." His mother swooped past him, her wings making a loud noise. He answered her with another scream. Then his father flew over him, screaming. Then he saw his two brothers and his sister flying around him curveting and banking and soaring and diving.

Then he completely forgot that he had not always been able to fly, and commenced himself to dive and soar and curvet, shrieking shrilly.

He was near the sea now, flying straight over it, facing straight out over the ocean. He saw a vast green sea beneath him, with little ridges moving over it, and he turned his beak sideways and crowed amusedly. His parents and his brothers and sister had landed on this green floor in front of him. They were beckoning to him, calling shrilly. He dropped his legs to stand on the green sea. His legs sank into it. He screamed with fright and attempted to rise again, flapping his wings. But he was tired and weak with hunger and he could not rise, exhausted by the strange exercise. His feet sank into the green sea, and then his belly touched it and he sank no farther. He was floating on it. And around him his family was screaming, praising him, and their beaks were offering him scraps of dog-fish. He had made his first flight.

Christmas Morning

Frank O'Connor

I never really liked my brother, Sonny. From the time he was a baby he was always the mother's pet and always chasing her to tell her what mischief I was up to. Mind you, I was usually up to something. Until I was nine or ten I was never much good at school, and I really believe it was to spite me that he was so smart at his books. He seemed to know by instinct that this was what Mother had set her heart on, and you might almost say he spelt himself into her favour.

"Mummy," he'd say, "will I call Larry in to his t-e-a?" or: "Mummy, the k-e-t-e-l is boiling," and, of course, when he was wrong she'd correct him, and next time he'd have it right and there would be no standing him. "Mummy," he'd say, "aren't I a good speller?" Cripes, we could all be good spellers if we went on like that!

Mind you, it wasn't that I was stupid. Far from it. I was just restless and not able to fix my mind for long on any one thing. I'd do the lessons for the year before, or the lessons for the year after: what I couldn't stand were the lessons we were supposed to be doing at the time. In the evenings I used to go out and play with the Doherty gang. Not, again, that I was rough, but I liked the excitement, and for the life of me I couldn't see what attracted Mother about education.

"Can't you do your lessons first and play after?" she'd say, getting white with indignation. "You ought to be ashamed of yourself that your baby brother can read better than you."

She didn't seem to understand that I wasn't, because there didn't seem to me to be anything particularly praiseworthy about reading, and it struck me as an occupation better suited to a sissy kid like Sonny.

97

"The dear knows what will become of you," she'd say. "If only you'd stick to your books you might be something good like a clerk or an engineer."

"I'll be a clerk, Mummy," Sonny would say smugly.

"Who wants to be an old clerk?" I'd say, just to annoy him. "I'm going to be a soldier."

"The dear knows, I'm afraid that's all you'll ever be fit for," she would add with a sigh.

I couldn't help feeling at times that she wasn't all there. As if there was anything better a fellow could be!

Coming on to Christmas, with the days getting shorter and the shopping crowds bigger, I began to think of all the things I might get from Santa Claus. The Dohertys said there was no Santa Claus, only what your father and mother gave you, but the Dohertys were a rough class of children you wouldn't expect Santa to come to anyway. I was rooting round for whatever information I could pick up about him, but there didn't seem to be much. I was no hand with a pen, but if a letter would do any good I was ready to chance writing to him. I had plenty of initiative and was always writing off for free samples and prospectuses.

"Ah, I don't know will he come at all this year," Mother said with a worried air. "He has enough to do looking after steady boys who mind their lessons without bothering about the rest."

"He only comes to good spellers, Mummy," said Sonny. "Isn't that right?"

"He comes to any little boy who does his best, whether he's a good speller or not," Mother said firmly.

Well, I did my best. God knows I did! It wasn't my fault if, four days before the holidays, Flogger Dawley gave us sums we couldn't do, and Peter Doherty and myself had to go on the lang. It wasn't for love of it, for, take it from me, December is no month for mitching, and we spent most of our time sheltering from the rain in a store on the quays. The only mistake we made was imagining we could keep it up till the holidays without being spotted. That showed real lack of foresight.

Of course, Flogger Dawley noticed and sent home word

98

to know what was keeping me. When I came in on the third day the mother gave me a look I'll never forget, and said: "Your dinner is there." She was too full to talk. When I tried to explain to her about Flogger Dawley and the sums she brushed it aside and said: "You have no word." I saw then it wasn't the langing she minded but the lies, though I still didn't see how you could lang without lying. She didn't speak to me for days. And even then I couldn't make out what she saw in education, or why she wouldn't let me grow up naturally like anyone else.

To make things worse, it stuffed Sonny up more than ever. He had the air of one saying: "I don't know what they'd do without me in this blooming house." He stood at the front door, leaning against the jamb with his hands in his trouser pockets, trying to make himself look like Father, and shouted to the other kids so that he could be heard all over the road.

"Larry isn't left go out. He went on the lang with Peter Doherty and me mother isn't talking to him."

And at night, when we were in bed, he kept it up.

"Santa Claus won't bring you anything this year, aha!"

"Of course he will," I said.

"How do you know?"

"Why wouldn't he?"

"Because you went on the lang with Doherty. I wouldn't play with them Doherty fellows."

"You wouldn't be left."

"I wouldn't play with them. They're no class. They had the bobbies up to the house."

"And how would Santa know I was on the lang with Peter Doherty?" I growled, losing patience with the little prig.

"Of course he'd know. Mummy would tell him."

"And how could Mummy tell him and he up at the North Pole. Poor Ireland, she's rearing them yet! 'Tis easy seen you're only an old baby."

"I'm not a baby, and I can spell better than you, and Santa won't bring you anything."

"We'll see whether he will or not," I said sarcastically,

99

doing the old man on him.

But, to tell the God's truth, the old man was only bluff. You could never tell what powers these superhuman chaps would have of knowing what you were up to. And I had a bad conscience about the langing because I'd never before seen the mother like that.

That was the night I decided that the only sensible thing to do was to see Santa myself and explain to him. Being a man, he'd probably understand. In those days I was a good-looking kid and had a way with me when I liked. I had only to smile nicely at one old gent on the North Mall to get a penny from him, and I felt if only I could get Santa by himself I could do the same with him and maybe get something worth while from him. I wanted a model railway: I was sick of Ludo and Snakes-and-Ladders.

I started to practise lying awake, counting five hundred and then a thousand, and trying to hear first eleven, then midnight, from Shandon. I felt sure Santa would be round by midnight, seeing that he'd be coming from the north, and would have the whole of the South Side to do afterwards. In some ways I was very far-sighted. The only trouble was the things I was far-sighted about.

I was so wrapped up in my own calculations that I had little attention to spare for Mother's difficulties. Sonny and I used to go to town with her, and while she was shopping we stood outside a toyshop in the North Main Street, arguing about what we'd like for Christmas.

On Christmas Eve when Father came home from work and gave her the housekeeping money, she stood looking at it doubtfully while her face grew white.

"Well?" he snapped, getting angry. "What's wrong with that?"

"What's wrong with it?" she muttered. "On Christmas Eve!"

"Well," he asked truculently, sticking his hands in his trouser pockets as though to guard what was left, "do you think I get more because it's Christmas?"

"Lord God," she muttered distractedly. "And not a bit of cake in the house, nor a candle, nor anything!"

"All right," he shouted, beginning to stamp. "How much will the candle be?"

"Ah, for pity's sake," she cried, "will you give me the money and not argue like that before the children? Do you think I'll leave them with nothing on the one day of the year?"

"Bad luck to you and your children!" he snarled. "Am I to be slaving from one year's end to another for you to be throwing it away on toys? Here," he added, tossing two half-crowns on the table, "that's all you're going to get, so make the most of it."

"I suppose the publicans will get the rest," she said bitterly.

Later she went into town, but did not bring us with her, and returned with a lot of parcels, including the Christmas candle. We waited for Father to come home to his tea, but he didn't, so we had our own tea and a slice of Christmas cake each, and then Mother put Sonny on a chair with the holy-water stoup to sprinkle the candle, and when he lit it she said: "The light of heaven to our souls." I could see she was upset because Father wasn't in—it should be the oldest and youngest. When we hung up our stockings at bedtime he was still out.

Then began the hardest couple of hours I ever put in. I was mad with sleep but afraid of losing the model railway, so I lay for a while, making up things to say to Santa when he came. They varied in tone from frivolous to grave. for some old gents like kids to be modest and well-spoken, while others prefer them with spirit. When I had rehearsed them all I tried to wake Sonny to keep me company, but that kid slept like the dead.

Eleven struck from Shandon, and soon after I heard the latch, but it was only Father coming home.

"Hello, little girl," he said, letting on to be surprised at finding Mother waiting up for him, and then broke into a self-conscious giggle. "What have you up so late?"

"Do you want your supper?" she asked shortly.

"Ah, no, no," he replied. "I had a bit of pig's cheek at Daneen's on my way up (Daneen was my uncle). I'm very

fond of a bit of pig's cheek.... My goodness, is it that late?"
he exclaimed, letting on to be astonished. "If I knew that
I'd have gone to the North Chapel for midnight Mass. I'd
like to hear the *Adeste* again. That's a hymn I'm very fond
of—a most touching hymn."

Then he began to hum it falsetto.

Adeste fideles
Solus domus dagus.

Father was very fond of Latin hymns, particularly when
he had a drop in, but as he had no notion of the words he
made them up as he went along, and this always drove
Mother mad.

"Ah, you disgust me!" she said in a scalded voice, and
closed the room door behind her. Father laughed as if he
thought it a great joke; and he struck a match to light his
pipe and for a while puffed at it noisily. The light under the
door dimmed and went out but he continued to sing
emotionally.

Dixie medearo
Tutum tonum tantum
Venite adoremus.

He had it all wrong but the effect was the same on me.
To save my life I couldn't keep awake.

Coming on to dawn, I woke with the feeling that something dreadful had happened. The whole house was quiet,
and the little bedroom that looked out on the foot and a
half of back yard was pitch-dark. It was only when I
glanced at the window that I saw how all the silver had
drained out of the sky. I jumped out of my bed to feel my
stocking, well knowing that the worst had happened. Santa
had come while I was asleep, and gone away with an
entirely false impression of me, because all he had left me
was some sort of book, folded up, a pen and pencil, and a
tuppenny bag of sweets. Not even Snakes-and-Ladders! For
a while I was too stunned even to think. A fellow who was
able to drive over rooftops and climb down chimneys
without getting stuck—God, wouldn't you think he'd know
better?

Then I began to wonder what that foxy boy, Sonny, had.

I went to his side of the bed and felt his stocking. For all his spelling and sucking-up he hadn't done so much better, because, apart from a bag of sweets like mine, all Santa had left him was a pop-gun, one that fired a cork on a piece of string and which you could get in any huxter's shop for sixpence.

All the same, the fact remained that it was a gun, and a gun was better than a book any day of the week. The Dohertys had a gang, and the gang fought the Strawberry Lane kids who tried to play football on our road. That gun would be very useful to me in many ways, while it would be lost on Sonny who wouldn't be let play with the gang, even if he wanted to.

Then I got the inspiration, as it seemed to me, direct from heaven. Suppose I took the gun and gave Sonny the book! Sonny would never be any good in the gang: he was fond of spelling, and a studious child like him could learn a lot of spellings from a book like mine. As he hadn't seen Santa any more than I had, what he hadn't seen wouldn't grieve him. I was doing no harm to anyone; in fact, if Sonny only knew, I was doing him a good turn which he might have cause to thank me for later. That was one thing I was always keen on; doing good turns. Perhaps this was Santa's intention the whole time and he had merely become confused between us. It was a mistake that might happen to anyone. So I put the book, the pencil, and the pen into Sonny's stocking and the popgun into my own, and returned to bed and slept again. As I say, in those days I had plenty of initiative.

It was Sonny who woke me, shaking me to tell me Santa had come and left me a gun. I let on to be surprised and rather disappointed in the gun, and to divert his mind from it made him show me his picture book, and cracked it up to the skies.

As I knew, that kid was prepared to believe anything, and nothing would do him then but to take the presents in to show Father and Mother. This was a bad moment for me. After the way she had behaved about the langing, I distrusted Mother, though I had the consolation of believing that the only person who could contradict me was now somewhere up by the North Pole. That gave me a certain confidence, so Sonny and I burst in with our presents, shouting: "Look what Santa Claus brought!"

Father and Mother woke, and Mother smiled, but only for an instant. As she looked at me her face changed. I knew that look; I knew it only too well. It was the same she had worn the day I came home from langing, when she said I had no word.

"Larry," she said in a low voice, "where did you get that gun?"

"Santa left it in my stocking, Mummy," I said, trying to put on an injured air, though it baffled me how she guessed that he hadn't. "He did, honest."

"You stole it from that poor child's stocking while he was asleep," she said, her voice quivering with indignation. "Larry, Larry, how could you be so mean?"

"Now, now, now," Father said deprecatingly, "'tis Christmas morning."

"Ah," she said with real passion, "it's easy it comes to you. Do you think I want my son to grow up a liar and a thief?"

"Ah, what thief, woman?" he said testily. "Have sense, can't you?" He was as cross if you interrupted him in his benevolent moods as if they were of the other sort, and this one was probably exacerbated by a feeling of guilt for his behaviour of the night before. "Here, Larry," he said, reaching out for the money on the bedside table, "here's sixpence for you and one for Sonny. Mind you don't lose it now!"

But I looked at Mother and saw what was in her eyes. I burst out crying, threw the popgun on the floor, and ran bawling out of the house before anyone on the road was awake. I rushed up the lane behind the house and threw myself on the wet grass.

I understood it all, and it was almost more than I could bear; that there was no Santa Claus, as the Dohertys said, only Mother trying to scrape together a few coppers from the housekeeping; that Father was mean and common and a drunkard, and that she had been relying on me to raise her out of the misery of the life she was leading. And I knew that the look in her eyes was the fear that, like my father, I should turn out to be mean and common and a drunkard.

Noulded into a Shake

Patrick Campbell

When I was a tall, sensitive boy at school I once sent up for a booklet about how to be a ventriloquist.

I was always 'sending up' for things—variable focus lamps, propelling pencils with choice of six differently-coloured leads, air-pistols discharging wooden bullets, scale model tanks with genuine caterpillar action, tricks in glass-topped boxes, and so on—anything, I suppose, to vary the monotony of straight games and education.

The booklet arrived at breakfast time one morning in a large square envelope. I told the other boys it was a new stamp album, and got on with my shredded liver poached in water. I wanted the voice-throwing to come as a real surprise.

We had twenty minutes after breakfast in which to get our things ready for first school. I had a quick run through the new book.

It was called *Ventriloquism in Three Weeks*. On the first page it explained that the word ventriloquism came from the Latin *ventriloqus*—'a speaking from the belly.' There was also a drawing of a schoolboy smiling pleasantly at a railway porter carrying a trunk. From the trunk came hysterical cries of, 'Help! Help! Murder! Police!'

It was just the sort of thing I was aiming at. I slipped the book in with my other ones, and hurried off to first school.

In the next fortnight I put in a good deal of practice, sitting right at the back of the class, watching my lips in a small piece of mirror, and murmuring, 'Dah, dee, day, di, doy, doo.'

It was necessary, however, to be rather careful. Dr Farvox, the author of the book, suggested that it might be as well to perform the earlier exercises 'in the privacy of one's bed-room or den.' Dr Farvox was afraid that 'chums or relatives'

106

might laugh, particularly while one was practising the 'muffled voice in the box.'

The best way to get this going, Dr Farvox said, was to experiment 'with a continuous grunting sound in a high key, straining from the chest as if in pain.'

He was right in thinking that this exercise ought to be performed in the privacy of the bedroom. It was inclined to be noisy—so noisy, indeed, that I was caught twice straining in a high key from the chest during practical chemistry, and had to pretend that I'd been overcome by the fumes of nitric acid.

But, in the end, it was the easy, pleasant smile that terminated my study of what Dr Farvox described as 'this amusing art.'

It happened one Saturday morning in the hour before lunch, ordinarily a pleasant enough period devoted to constitutional history. Bill the Bull, who took the class, was usually fairly mellow with the prospect of the week-end before him, and there was not much need to do any work.

As was by now my invariable custom I was seated right at the back of the room with a large pile of books in front of me, and the mirror lying on the desk. I was working on the Whisper Voice, which had been giving me quite a considerable amount of difficulty.

'Lie down, Neddy, lie down," I whispered, watching my lips closely in the glass.

"It's due in dock at nine o'clock."

Not bad.

"Take Ted's Kodak down to Roy."

There it was again—the old familiar twitch on 'Kodak.'

I sat back, relaxing a little, and smiled. Dr Farvox was strongly in favour of the Smile. "What the young student," he said, "should aim at from the first is an easy and natural expression. He should Smile."

I smiled. Smiling, I whispered, "Take Ted's Kodak down to Roy."

To my absolute horror I found myself smiling straight into the face of Bill the Bull.

He stopped dead. He was in the middle of something

107

about the growth of common law, but my smile stopped him dead in his tracks.

"Well, well," said Bill, after a moment. "How charming. And good morning to you, too."

I at once buried my face in my books, and tried to shove the mirror and *Ventriloquism in Three Weeks* on one side.

Bill rolled slowly down the passageway between the desks. He was an enormous Welshman with a bullet head, and very greasy, straight black hair. He took a subtle and delicate pleasure in driving the more impressionable amongst us half mad with fear at least five days a week.

"Such pretty teeth," said Bill. "How nice of you to smile at me. I have always wanted to win your admiration."

The other boys sat back. They knew they were on to something good.

I kept my head lowered. I'd actually succeeded in opening my constitutional history somewhere near the middle, but the corner of Dr Farvox was clearly visible under a heap of exercise books.

Bill reached my desk. "But who knows," he said, "perhaps you love me too. Perchance you've been sitting there all morning just dreaming of a little home—just you and I. And later, perhaps, some little ones...?"

A gasp of incredulous delight came from the other boys. This was Bill at his very best.

I looked up. It was no longer possible to pretend I thought he was talking to someone else.

"I'm sorry, sir," I said. "I was just smiling."

Suddenly, Bill pounced. He snatched up Dr Farvox.

"Cripes," he said. "What in the world have we here? Ventroliquism in three weeks?"

He turned a couple of pages.

"Scholars," he said, "be so good as to listen to this."

He read aloud: "To imitate a Fly. Close the lips tight at one corner. Fill that cheek full of wind and force it to escape through the aperture. Make the sound suddenly loud, and then softer, which will make it appear as though the insect were flying in different parts of the room. The illusion may be helped out by the performer chasing the

108

imaginary fly, and flapping at it with his handkerchief."

"Strewth," said Bill. He looked round the class. "We'd better get ourselves a little bit of this. Here am I taking up your time with the monotonies of constitutional history, while in this very room we have a trained performer who can imitate a fly."

Suddenly, he caught me by the back of the neck. "Come," he said, "my little love, and let us hear this astounding impression."

He dragged me down to the dais.

"Begin," said Bill. "Be so kind as to fill your cheek with wind, and at all costs do not omit the flapping of the handkerchief."

"Sir," I said, "that's animal noises. I haven't got that far yet."

"Sir," squeaked Bill, in a high falsetto, "that's animal noises. I 'aven't got that far yet."

He surveyed the convulsed class calmly.

"Come, come," he said, "this art is not as difficult as I had imagined it to be. Did anyone see my lips move?"

They cheered him. They banged the lids of their desks. "Try it again, sir!" they cried. "It's splendid!"

Bill raised his hand. "Gentlemen," he said, "I thank you for your kindness. I am, however, but an amateur. Am I not right in thinking that we would like to hear something more from Professor Smallpox?"

They cheered again. Someone shouted, "Make him sing a song, sir!"

Bill turned to me. "Can you," he said, "Professor Smallpox, sing a song?"

It was the worst thing that had ever happened to me in my life. I tried to extricate myself.

"No, sir," I said. "I haven't mastered the labials yet."

Bill started back. He pressed his hand to his heart.

"No labials?" he said. "You have reached the age of fifteen without having mastered the labials. But, dear Professor Smallpox, we must look into this. Perhaps you would be so kind as to give us some outline of your difficulties?"

I picked up *Ventriloquism in Three Weeks.* There was no way out.

"There's a sentence here, sir, that goes, 'A pat of butter moulded into the shape of a boat.' "

Bill inclined his head. "Is there, indeed? A most illuminating remark. You propose to put it to music?"

"No, sir," I said. "I'm just trying to show you how hard it is. You see, you have to call that, 'A cat of gutter noulded into the shake of a goat.' "

Bill fell right back into his chair.

"You have to call it *what?*" he said.

"A cat of gutter, sir, noulded into the shake of a goat."

Bill's eyes bulged. "Professor," he said, "you astound me. You bewilder me. You take my breath away. A cat of gutter—" He repeated it reverently, savouring each individual syllable.

Then he sprang up. "But we must hear this," he cried. "We must have this cat of gutter delivered by someone who knows what he is at. This—this is valuable stuff."

He caught me by the ear. "Professor," he said, "why does it have to be noulded into the shake of a goat?"

"Well, sir," I said, "if you say it like that you don't have to move your lips. You sort of avoid the labials."

"To be sure you do," said Bill. "Why didn't I think of that myself. Well, now, we will have a demonstration."

He turned to face the class. "Gentlemen," he said, "Professor Smallpox will now say, 'A pat of butter moulded into the shape of a boat,' *without moving the lips!* I entreat your closest attention. You have almost certainly never in your lives heard anything like this before."

He picked up his heavy ebony ruler. His little pig-like eyes gleamed.

"And," he went on, "to make sure that Professor Smallpox will really give us of his best I shall make it my personal business to give Professor Smallpox a clonk on the conk with this tiny weapon should any of you see even the faintest movement of the facial muscles as he delivers his unforgettable message."

Bill brought down the ruler with a sharp crack on my

skull.

"Professor," he said, "it's all yours."

I don't have to go into the next twenty-five minutes. The other boys yelled practically on every syllable. I got the meaningless words tangled up, and said, "A cack of rutter roulded into the gake of a shote."

At times Bill was so helpless with laughter that he missed me with the ruler altogether.

When the bell went for the end of the hour he insisted on being helped out into the passage, wiping his eyes with the blackboard cloth.

After that, I gave up ventriloquism, feeling no recurrence of interest even after reading Bill's observation on my end-of-term report: 'He ought to do well on the stage.'

The Editor's thanks are due to the following for permission to use their short stories:

Jonathan Cape Ltd, for "His First Flight" from *The Short Stories of Liam O'Flaherty;* John Farquharson Ltd, for "One of the Virtues" by Stan Barstow; William Heinemann Ltd, for "Vanity" from *The Saturdays* by Elizabeth Enright; Irene Josephy, for "Noulded into a Shake" from *The P-P-Penguin Patrick Campbell;* Macmillan & Co. Ltd, The Macmillan Company of Canada Ltd, St Martin's Press Inc., for "The Magpie" by Alan Jenkins from *Winter's Tales for Children 4,* edited by M. R. Hodgkin; Oxford University Press, for "The Mersey Look" by Eric Allen from *Miscellany One,* edited by Edward Blishen; Pergamon Press Ltd, for "The Bachelor Uncle" by Sid Chaplin; A. D. Peters & Co., for "Zero Hour" by Ray Bradbury from *S is for Space,* and for "Christmas Morning" from *Stories of Frank O'Connor;* Laurence Pollinger Ltd, for "Adolf" by D. H. Lawrence from *Phoenix.*